FRIGHTMARES

Desert Danger

D0645751

Books by Peg Kehret

Cages
Horror at the Haunted House
Nightmare Mountain
Sisters, Long Ago
Terror at the Zoo
Frightmares™: Cat Burglar on the Prowl
Frightmares™: Bone Breath and the Vandals
Frightmares™: Don't Go Near Mrs. Tallie
Frightmares™: Desert Danger

Available from MINSTREL Books

FRIGHTMARES™

Desert Danger

Peg Kehret

A MINSTREL® HARDCOVER
PUBLISHED BY POCKET BOOKS
New York London Toronto Sydney Tokyo Singapore

A MINSTREL HARDCOVER

 A Minstrel Book published by
POCKET BOOKS, a division of Simon & Schuster Inc.
1230 Avenue of the Americas, New York, NY 10020

Kehret, Peg.
    Desert danger / Peg Kehret.
        p.   cm. — (Frightmares; #4)
    "A Minstrel hardcover."
    Summary: Rosie and Kayo's new Care Club project leads to a
frightening kidnapping.
    ISBN 978-1-4169-9111-3
    ISBN 1-416-99111-5

    [1. Kidnapping—Fiction. 2. Clubs—Fiction.] I. Title.
II. Series: Kehret, Peg. Frightmares; #4.
PZ7.K2815Der   1995
[Fic]—dc20   94-46570
                                                         CIP
                                                          AC

First Minstrel Books hardcover printing October 1995

10 9 8 7 6 5 4 3 2 1

For Anne,
for so many reasons

FRIGHTMARES™

Desert Danger

CARE CLUB
We Care About Animals

I. Whereas we, the undersigned, care about our animal friends, we promise to groom them, play with them, and exercise them daily. We will do this for the following animals:

> **WEBSTER** (Rosie's cat)
> **BONE BREATH** (Rosie's dog)
> **HOMER** (Kayo's cat)
> **DIAMOND** (Kayo's cat)

II. Whereas we, the undersigned, care about the well-being of *all* creatures, we promise to do whatever we can to help homeless animals.

III. Care Club will hold official meetings every Thursday afternoon or whenever else there is important business. All Care Club projects will be for the good of the animals.

Signed:

Rosie Saunders

Kayo Benton

Chapter

Kayo Benton kicked a stone. It was the last day to turn in the registration form for Sixth Grade Baseball Camp, and her dad, as usual, had failed to send a check.

Mom warned me not to get my hopes up, Kayo thought bitterly as she walked to Rosie's house for the Care Club meeting. *Dad hasn't sent a support check for two years; what made me think he'd come through with some money now, just because I wrote and explained how important it is for me to go to Baseball Camp?*

She caught up to the stone and kicked it again. *He knows I want to be a professional baseball player. Kick. Baseball Camp isn't just a way to waste some time next summer. Kick, kick.*

Kayo's *Field of Dreams* sweatshirt, her birth-

1

day present from Rosie, hung loosely on her tall, slender frame as she walked on. She wondered if her father's two stepchildren, who lived with him, would go to camp this summer.

Probably, she decided. They see him every day. They probably go to camp and take music lessons and ride their very own pony and wear all the latest fashions, including eighty-dollar running shoes.

She kicked another stone, harder this time. If she was going to be a major league baseball player, she needed the proper training.

Forget about it, her mother had said. It isn't worth getting so upset over something you can't control.

She couldn't forget, not when all the other kids on her team were turning in their registration forms and their money. It wasn't fair. Kayo was the best player on her team. How could her own father ignore her this way, as if she didn't matter?

Rosie greeted her at the door, bouncing with excitement. "You'll never guess what's happened!" she said and then, without waiting for Kayo to ask "What?" she rushed on. "Mom and Dad bought a mini motor home and we're taking it to Arizona over spring break!"

Usually Kayo was not an envious person. Most days she would have been delighted for Rosie.

But right then, with her spirits as low as a fast-ball in the dirt, all she could think was, oh, no. Not only do I have to miss Baseball Camp, but Rosie will be gone during spring break and I won't have anything to do that whole week.

Kayo's lack of response didn't slow Rosie down. "It has a refrigerator," she said, "and a little bathroom, and a closet that smells like cedar. It even has a microwave. We can make popcorn! We get it tomorrow and we leave as soon as school is out on Friday. We'll be gone nine days."

Kayo forced a smile, trying to look enthusiastic. "It sounds great," she said.

Rosie raced on. "It will be so much fun! Bone Breath is going with us, but our next door neighbor is going to take care of Webster because we're afraid he'd meow the whole time we're driving, like he does when he goes to the vet for his shots. Mom and Dad will sleep on the regular bed; they bought a double sleeping bag. You and I get the bed that folds down from the sofa. Do you have a sleeping bag? If you don't, you can borrow Toby's. He won't be going with us because his spring break from college is a different time."

"Wait a minute," Kayo said. "*I'm* sleeping on the sofa bed? *I* need a sleeping bag?"

"Yes! That's the best part," Rosie said. "I told

Mom and Dad I would die of boredom unless you came with us, and Dad said he doesn't have time to plan my funeral, so you get to come."

An astonished smile crept across Kayo's face.

"We're going to go to a baseball game while we're in Phoenix," Rosie added. "Dad says he's always wanted to see a Cactus League game and this is his chance."

"Cactus League?" Kayo said. "We're going to a baseball game during spring training?" A thrill of excitement swept down her arms and legs. Never, even in her wildest daydreams, had Kayo thought she would attend a spring training game. How could she? The major league teams hold their spring training games in Arizona or Florida, and the only way she and her mom could afford to go would be to sprout wings and fly South themselves.

"Dad said since you play baseball, you would like to see a game, so he's getting tickets for all of us."

"Like to?" Kayo said. "*Like* to?" She clamped both hands on her head, pressing her San Diego Padres cap into her long blond hair. "Would I like to win the lottery?" she cried. "Would I like to find an oil well in my backyard?" She grabbed Rosie and hugged her. "Your dad," she said, "is

4

terrific! I'm going to nominate him for Father of the Year."

"What about me?" Rosie said. "Aren't you going to nominate me for Friend of the Year?"

"You," said Kayo, "are Friend of the Decade. You are Friend of the Century. Spring training in Arizona! Wait till I tell my coach!"

A week later the Saunderses' motor home rolled into the Usery Mountain Recreation Area. Kayo and Rosie looked up at the word PHOENIX, which stood out in white letters, high on a hill.

"I hope I make it to the baseball game," Kayo said.

"Why wouldn't you make it?" Rosie asked.

"I may die of happiness before then," Kayo replied.

"You can't," Mr. Saunders said. "I've already paid for your ticket." He stopped at the Usery Mountain campground entrance and took a registration slip.

When Jasper Dodge registered at Usery Mountain campground, he signed a false name. He paid with cash, so there would be no record of the payment. As he wrote down the license plate number of the rented truck, he transposed a number, on purpose. There was no way anyone could trace him.

The red pickup with a black camper mounted on the back had everything Jasper needed: small size for a quick getaway, curtains on the windows, and a door that locked from the outside, with a key, so it could not be opened from within. Once he had the girl, she would not escape.

Jasper wasn't as pleased with his assistant as he was with the vehicle. Benny had the brainpower of a fly, and maybe that was an insult to the flies. But Benny was a muscular boxer, trained in karate, and those skills might come in handy.

Jasper would not need Benny for long. He intended to take the girl, collect the ransom, and leave the country. Fast. After he paid Benny, Jasper would never see him again.

"Look at all the cactuses," Kayo said as they drove into the campground.

"Cacti," corrected Rosie. "The plural of *cactus* is *cacti*."

"Is that your vocabulary word for this week?" Kayo asked.

Rosie shook her head. "That would be too easy. We'll be saying *cacti* anyway."

Desert Danger

Cactuses sounded better to Kayo than *cacti,* but she didn't say so. Rosie was fussy about words.

Rosie's cairn terrier, Bone Breath, sat on Kayo's lap, making nose prints on the window. He seemed as interested in the desert as she was.

As soon as they were parked in their campsite, Rosie and Kayo took Bone Breath for a walk. Cactus plants grew on both sides of the road. Some, taller than the girls, stretched their spiny arms toward the sky. Others, short and round, squatted on the ground like fat pincushions.

Stretches of desert separated the large campsites. Wildflowers bloomed. Quail called from the shadows.

"I thought the desert would be nothing but sand," Rosie said. "This place is beautiful."

A wooden sign, NATURE TRAIL, marked a narrow path which led away from the paved road. The girls turned onto the trail. Bone Breath tugged eagerly at his leash.

"Look!" Rosie said, pointing. "There are markers to identify the plants. This one is called prickly pear. Instead of having a vocabulary word this week, let's learn the names of all the desert plants."

Kayo agreed. Usually she didn't get excited about Rosie's plan to learn a new vocabulary word each week and use it five times daily in conversation, but it would be fun to know the names of all the cactuses. Oops. She mentally corrected herself: cacti.

Rosie pointed at the sand around the next sign. "Pieces of the chain fruit cholla have dropped off. They're all over the ground."

They saw a short hedgehog cactus and a fat, round barrel cactus. The next sign said PACK RAT NEST. At the base of a prickly pear, a tangle of cactus roots, twigs, and dried up cactus branches stretched three feet across the ground. Holes served as entrances and exits.

As the girls stared at the pack rat nest, a rabbit hopped across the path a few yards ahead of them.

Bone Breath yelped and took off after the rabbit. The sudden movement jerked Rosie off the trail.

She collided with a chain fruit cholla. The sleeve of her T-shirt clung to the cactus; the sharp spines pierced the fabric and poked into Rosie's arm.

"Ouch!" she cried. "Kayo, I'm stuck!"

Bone Breath yipped and tugged at the leash.

"I'll take Bone Breath," Kayo said, reaching for the leash. Using both hands, she controlled the excited dog and got him safely back on the trail beside her.

Rosie's arm felt as if it were on fire. When she tried to pull free from the cholla, a piece of the cactus broke off the main plant and stuck to her arm. The tips of the spines jabbed through her skin like a handful of needles.

Rosie bit her lip to keep from crying. She took her vocabulary notebook from her pocket and used it to protect her hand as she pushed the clump of cholla loose. Several spines, each more than an inch long, broke off the plant and stayed in Rosie's arm. One at a time she grasped the ends and yanked them out.

When they were all gone, she pulled up her sleeve and looked at her arm. Small red welts remained where each spine had broken the skin, and her whole upper arm was swollen and tender.

"That hurts," Rosie said as she removed her glasses and wiped a tear from the corner of her eye.

"If Bone Breath is going to bolt after rabbits," Kayo said, "we should keep him on the paved road in the camping area. This trail is too narrow." She shortened the leash and held it with both hands while they returned to their campsite.

As they approached the motor home, Bone Breath barked again.

"Hush, Bone Breath," Rosie said.

Bone Breath tugged eagerly forward, wagging his tail.

"He probably sees another rabbit," Kayo said.

Bone Breath stopped beside the motor home and stared underneath it, yipping with excitement.

Kayo got down on one knee and looked. "Rosie!" she said. "There's a baby kitten under the motor home."

Chapter

"Meow."

The kitten stretched and looked at them. It was black with a white chest and three white feet.

The girls put Bone Breath inside and then knelt down and peered under the motor home.

"Here, kitty," Rosie said softly. "Here, kitty, kitty." She held her hand toward the kitten.

The kitten walked toward the girls. It stopped to sniff Rosie's fingers and then came out from under the motor home, its tiny tail straight up like a flagpole.

Kayo picked the kitten up and held it against her chest. The kitten tucked its head down and began to purr.

"It's a friendly little thing," Kayo said. "I wonder who it belongs to."

Rosie petted the kitten for a moment. "We'd better try to find its owner," she said. "It's too little to be wandering around alone."

Mr. and Mrs. Saunders walked down the path from the rest rooms, carrying towels and bottles of shampoo.

"Mom! Dad!" Rosie called. "We found a kitty."

Rosie's parents hurried toward the girls. "We aren't keeping it," Mr. Saunders said. "Not in the motor home."

"It can't be more than six weeks old," Mrs. Saunders said. "We'd better give it some milk."

"We aren't keeping it," Mr. Saunders repeated.

"Of course we aren't," Mrs. Saunders said. "But we aren't going to let it starve to death, either."

Bone Breath went wild when they carried the kitten inside. He jumped from the floor to the sofa and back to the floor, wagging his tail and trying to smell the cat. The kitten arched its back and hissed.

Rosie shut Bone Breath in the bathroom while Kayo poured a small saucer of milk. The kitten lapped it eagerly and then sat on the sofa, washing her whiskers.

"Out of all the occupied campsites in this park," Mr. Saunders said, "why did the cat hide under our motor home?"

"Animals know when people like them," Rosie said.

Bone Breath whined pitifully from the bathroom.

"We'll take it to the campground hosts," Mr. Saunders said. "They should know if someone is looking for it."

Rosie picked up the kitten. It wriggled out of her hands and ran into the narrow space behind the sofa.

"You girls can't carry that skittery kitten around the campground," Mrs. Saunders said. "Leave it here with us while you go tell the campground hosts that you found it."

The girls hurried down the road. They had seen the large trailer with the sign CAMPGROUND HOSTS in one of the first campsites.

Rosie knocked on the door. A smiling gray-haired woman answered. "What can I do for you?" she asked.

"We found a lost kitten," Kayo asked.

The woman's smile faded. "Oh, no," she said. "Not another one."

Kayo and Rosie looked at each other.

"Come inside, girls," the woman said. "My name is Marie Harris and this is my husband, Paul."

A chunky man in a red plaid shirt sat in a chair

behind her, reading a book. He did not look up when they entered.

"These girls found a kitten," Mrs. Harris said.

The man sighed and closed his book. "Again?" he said.

"Again?" said Rosie. "Has the kitten been lost before?"

"I doubt it's a lost pet," Mrs. Harris said.

"It's a throwaway cat," her husband said. "Happens all the time. Someone in town has a litter of kittens and they can't find homes for them all so they bring the leftovers up here to the park and dump them."

"That's terrible!" Rosie said.

"People think cats can survive on their own in the wild," Mrs. Harris said. "We have a lot of mice up here; they figure the cats will eat mice."

"What they don't realize," Mr. Harris said, "is that we also have coyotes who think a tender little kitten is a tasty snack."

Rosie and Kayo glanced at each other, horrified.

"If the coyotes don't get them," Mrs. Harris said, "they either starve to death, get hit by a car, or die of disease. When cats don't get vaccinated and they're without shelter and decent food, they get sick easily." She shook her head sadly. "People are so cruel."

"Stupid!" Mr. Harris said. "That's what they are—just plain stupid! There are places to take unwanted animals where they'll be treated kindly and have a chance to get a good home, but no, people bring them up here and throw them out to die."

"What are we going to do?" Rosie said. "My parents said I can't keep the kitten."

"We'll post a Lost notice on the camp bulletin board," Mrs. Harris said. "I don't expect it to do any good, though. If people had lost a kitten, they would be looking for it. I walked all around the campground only an hour ago, and no one was out calling a kitty."

Mr. Harris said, "If you girls want to, you can go around to the campsites and ask if anyone would like to adopt a kitten. Last year some people from Indiana took a throwaway cat home with them. Maybe you'll get lucky and find this one a good home."

"You don't *have* to do that, of course," Mrs. Harris added. "The kitten isn't your responsibility."

"Oh, we'll do it," Kayo said. "We have a club, Care Club, and one of our goals is to help homeless animals."

"That one is certainly homeless," Mr. Harris said.

"If you don't find someone who wants a cat," Mrs. Harris said, "bring it here. We'll take it in to the animal shelter. That way, if it doesn't get adopted, it will be put painlessly to sleep."

The girls thanked the hosts for their help and left.

"We have to find a home for the kitty," Kayo said. "We can't let them take it to the shelter."

"Throwaway cat," Rosie said. "What an awful phrase."

"It sounds as if the kitten is a piece of garbage, like a banana peel."

"Even if the people didn't want to keep her themselves, you'd think they would see that she got a decent home. How can they just walk away and forget about her?"

"It happens," Kayo said softly. "And not just to cats. My own father walked away and forgot about me." She had never told anyone, not even Rosie, how she felt about her father's lack of interest, but now, with her emotions already stirred up by the abandoned kitten, her thoughts just blurted out.

The words hung in the air as if she'd pinned them on a clothesline, and, once spoken, the thought seemed more terrible and more real.

"Oh, Kayo," Rosie said. "You weren't abandoned. Your dad knows you have a good home;

he knows your mom is there to watch out for you. Just because he doesn't send any support money doesn't mean he's forgotten you. I'll bet he thinks about you a lot, but he's too busy to write letters or call."

Kayo was not convinced. Throwaway girl, she thought. As far as my father is concerned, I'm only a piece of garbage.

"Let's name the kitten," Rosie said. "That will show someone cares about her."

"How about Banana Peel?"

"No! How can you say that?"

"I'm sorry," Kayo said. "I get depressed when I talk about my dad."

"Then let's not talk about him. We have better things to do, like find a home for—for Phoenix."

"Phoenix?"

"Yes. Let's name her Phoenix."

"Good idea," Kayo said. "We found her here. She was probably born in Phoenix."

"And," Rosie said, "the early Greeks had a mythical bird named Phoenix that lived to be five hundred years old. When it finally died, it was cremated and a new young bird flew up out of the ashes. The word *phoenix* is a symbol for everlasting life, and I hope the kitten lives a long, long time."

"How do you know stuff like that?" Kayo said.

17

Rosie shrugged. "I read a lot."

"It's a perfect name."

When the girls got back to the motor home, the dishpan was filled with sand, gathered from the campsite. Phoenix was curled on a bath towel on the sofa. Bone Breath lay beside her, panting and wagging his tail.

"She ate some tuna," Mrs. Saunders said, "but we'll have to buy cat food tomorrow. Tuna is too rich for her."

"We also need litter," Mr. Saunders said. "I'm not shoveling any more sand from the campground. It's probably illegal. I'll be thrown in jail and miss the ball game."

"That would make headlines," Kayo said. "Famous cartoonist arrested for stealing public property."

"I'll represent you in court," Mrs. Saunders said.

"We named the kitten Phoenix," Rosie said.

"That's appropriate," Mr. Saunders said. "This cat has used at least one of her nine lives."

Rosie's parents agreed that the girls should go around and ask if anyone had lost a kitten or wanted to adopt one.

"Be back in an hour," Mrs. Saunders said. "We're eating dinner out on the picnic table."

"I never thought we'd find a Care Club project

in Arizona," Rosie said as they headed off to talk to other campers.

"This time I hope we don't end up screaming for help, like we have with every other official project."

"Don't even say it," Rosie said.

Chapter 3

No, thanks. I have two cats at home."

"Sorry. I'm allergic to cat fur."

"I can't afford another pet."

Rosie and Kayo spoke with people in eight other campsites. All were sympathetic and said they hoped the girls would find a home for Phoenix. None of them offered to take the little cat.

One older couple sat in green lawn chairs outside a large fifth wheeler. A wooden sign on their door said THE WILBERTS. They were furious when they heard how someone had dumped Phoenix in the park.

"We had a cat for eighteen years," Mr. Wilbert said. "Bumpkins liked to travel; he went with us everywhere. We always said he was probably the only cat who had been in forty-five states. Just yesterday we said we still miss our Baby Bumpkins."

His wife nodded. "It was so hard on us when he passed on. We cried for weeks."

"Our little granddaughter was heartbroken, too," Mr. Wilbert said. "Bumpkins used to sleep with Susie when she visited us."

Mrs. Wilbert opened a gold locket which hung on a chain around her neck. She held it up so Kayo and Rosie could see the pictures inside the locket. "This is Susie," she said, "and this is Bumpkins."

The little girl looked about four; the cat was black with a white chest.

"He looks a lot like the kitten we found," Rosie said. "The kitten is black with a white bib and three white feet."

"Bumpkins had three white feet, too," Mrs. Wilbert said. "We always joked that Puss had lost one of his boots." She turned the locket so she could see the pictures herself. "Did you hear that, Will?" she said. "Their kitten looks like our Bumpkins."

"We agreed," Mr. Wilbert said, "never to put ourselves through such grief again. No more cats."

Mrs. Wilbert sighed. "You're right," she said and snapped the locket shut.

"If you change your minds," Kayo said, "we're parked in site number twenty-eight."

"We'll think about it," the woman said.

"Now, Mother . . ." the man said.

As the girls walked on, Kayo whispered, "I think they might change their minds, don't you?"

"I hope so," Rosie said.

They talked with several other people before it was time for dinner. No one wanted a kitten.

"Any luck?" Mr. Saunders said when they returned to the motor home.

"No," said Kayo. She scooped the kitten into her lap and stroked the soft fur. Phoenix purred and stuck her front claws in and out of Kayo's jeans.

"I was afraid of that," Mr. Saunders said. "Who would be crazy enough to adopt a kitten when they're traveling?"

"Us?" said Rosie hopefully.

"No. Not us," Mr. Saunders said. "Not when we already have a dog along. To say nothing of Webster waiting at home. Remember how Webster acted when you brought Mrs. Tallie's cat home, when Mrs. Tallie was ill? None of us got any sleep for days."

Rosie remembered. Webster had terrorized the other cat and put Bone Breath in a frenzy of barking. Fortunately, Mrs. Tallie recovered and took Muffin home.

"Could we stay here again tomorrow night?" Rosie asked as she helped carry dishes out to the picnic table.

"We plan to stay closer to the ball park tomorrow night," Mrs. Saunders said. "Peoria Stadium is on the other side of town."

"But we have to come back here," Rosie said.

"What difference does it make if it's this campground or one closer to the stadium?"

"We talked to one couple—they look kind of like Grandma and Grandpa—who said they would think it over. Their cat died and they miss it a lot and they might decide to take Phoenix. If we aren't here, they wouldn't know how to contact us."

"They probably just said that so you wouldn't feel bad," Mr. Saunders said. "If they wanted a cat, they would have taken her right then."

"Their cat was named Bumpkins," Kayo said, "and they cried for weeks when she died. I know they'd be good to Phoenix, if they take her."

"It would be a shame to take the kitty somewhere else," Mrs. Saunders said, "if there's a chance that someone here wants her."

"Please, Dad?" Rosie said.

Mr. Saunders rolled his eyes. "I can see I'm

outvoted," he said. "All right. We'll come back here tomorrow night."

Rosie hugged her father. "Thanks," she said.

Over her shoulder, Mr. Saunders complained to Kayo, "I should know better than to travel with my daughter." But he smiled as he said it, and he kissed Rosie's cheek.

Watching them, Kayo got a lump in her throat. Why couldn't her dad be like Mr. Saunders?

"Finding a home for Phoenix is an official Care Club project," Rosie said.

"Oh, no," Mr. Saunders said. "Every time you two have a Care Club project, you end up in trouble."

"I still get nightmares," Mrs. Saunders said, "when I think about you in that Dumpster."

"Worse than nightmares," Mr. Saunders said. "Frightmares."

"We won't leave the campground," Rosie said. "What can happen to us, just walking around camp?"

"Probably nothing," Mrs. Saunders admitted.

The girls ate quickly.

"You can be excused from doing dishes tonight," Mrs. Saunders said. "It's more important to find a home for the kitten."

"Be back here before dark," Mr. Saunders warned.

"We will," Rosie promised.

They hurried past the campsites where they had already talked to someone.

As they approached a huge silver motor home, Kayo said, "This one is bigger than my whole apartment. I wonder how they ever park it."

When they knocked, a girl their own age answered.

"Did you lose a kitten?" Rosie asked.

"I don't have any pets," the girl said. "I love animals, but we travel a lot for my dad's business, and it's too hard to find someone to care for a pet when we're away."

"Why can't you take your pet with you?" Rosie asked. "We have my dog with us, and our motor home is lots smaller than yours."

"We usually fly," the girl said. "And with many countries, there's a waiting period of several weeks when your animal has to stay in quarantine."

"You've been to other countries?" Rosie said.

"So far, I've been to France, England, Brazil, Australia, and Switzerland. My dad has offices all over the world."

Kayo stared at the girl. She had never met someone who had traveled to other countries.

The girl smiled. "I hope you find the kitten's owner," she said.

"To tell you the truth," Rosie said, "we don't

expect to find the owner. We think the kitten was abandoned. We hope to find someone who will adopt it."

"Do you want me to help you?"

"That would be great," Kayo said. "We're going to all the campsites, asking if anyone lost a cat. Then, if they seem like nice people, we ask if they want to take the kitten."

"If they say yes," Rosie said, "my mother will come and talk to them, to be sure they really will give it a good home. She says we have to be careful or someone might say they want a pet but they really plan to do something horrible, like sell it to a place that uses animals for experiments."

The girl shuddered.

"Mom's an attorney," Rosie added. "She's good at questioning people and figuring out their motives."

"If you come with us," Kayo said, "you could ask on one side of the road while we do the other. We'd get done a lot faster."

"Let me leave a note for my parents," the girl said. "Dad is in town at a computer convention, and Mom is sitting in the desert somewhere with her binoculars, watching birds."

Seconds later she came out, wearing a windbreaker. "I'm Elisabeth Lynwood," she said.

Kayo and Rosie introduced themselves. "We're in sixth grade," Rosie said.

"Me, too." Elisabeth was tall and slender, like Kayo. Her blond hair was pulled back in two ponytails.

As the three girls walked away from Elisabeth's big silver motor home, Rosie and Kayo told her about their Care Club.

Jasper Dodge drove slowly through the campground, looking carefully at each vehicle.

"What if they aren't here yet?" Benny asked.

"We'll wait."

"How long?"

"Until they get here," Jasper snapped. "For five thousand dollars, you can afford to wait." And I can afford to wait, too, Jasper thought. He was paying Benny five thousand, but Jasper's own share of the ransom would be more than that. Much more.

Personally, Jasper didn't think there was a kid in the world who was worth one hundred thousand dollars, but he knew he would get every dime. Andrew Lynwood thought the sun rose and set on his kid. She was his only child, his princess, and he would pay the money, all right. All of it.

"There's a big one," Benny said, pointing to

the silver motor home that was parked in a campsite ahead.

Jasper read the personal license plate: LYN-WOOD. He felt a stirring of excitement, the way he always felt when he was about to make a pile of money.

The next campsite down, across the road from the silver motor home, was vacant.

"The Lynwoods now have neighbors," Jasper said. "I'll back in so we can pull out fast if we need to." He backed into the campsite, turned off the engine, and tossed the keys to Benny.

They got out and walked around the campsite, looking across the road toward the Lynwood's motor home.

Jasper sat at the picnic table. "Here's our spot," he said. "I can see the entrance to their campsite. I can even see their door; we'll know who comes and goes."

"What if Andrew Lynwood recognizes you?" Benny asked.

"He won't. I lost thirty pounds in prison, and when I worked for him, I had a beard. Besides, Andrew Lynwood won't see me. Only his daughter will see me."

They played gin rummy and waited.

"Someone's coming," Benny said.

Jasper turned slightly and looked over his

shoulder. "It's his wife," he said. "He always had her picture on his desk."

Mrs. Lynwood took keys from her pocket, opened the door, and went inside. A few minutes later she came out, wearing running shorts and a headband. She put both hands on the side of the motor home and stretched her leg muscles. Then she jogged down the road and ran out of sight.

"If the kid shows up now," Jasper said, "Mama won't hear or see anything."

Chapter

The western sky glowed red. Rosie, Kayo, and Elisabeth paused to admire the black silhouettes of the cacti against the sunset. They had visited fifteen campsites, but the kitten was still homeless.

"Those two saguaro look thirty feet tall," Rosie said. She took her vocabulary notebook out of her pocket and made a check mark, to show she had used a new word.

For once, Kayo knew what Rosie meant the first time she used a new vocabulary word.

"Which ones are saguaro?" Elisabeth asked.

"The tall ones," Rosie said, "with their arms in the air like people in an exercise class."

"There's a nature trail," Kayo said, "with signs that tell what all the plants are. That's how we learned the names."

"That sounds fun," Elisabeth said. "I've been wondering what those little fat ones are."

"Hedgehog cactus," Kayo replied. "They're my favorites."

"We'll show you where the trail is," Rosie said. "We saw holes high up in one cactus, as if birds nest inside."

Kayo and Rosie led the way to where the trail branched off the main part of the road. They showed Elisabeth the signs and the pack rat's nest.

"Yuck," Elisabeth said. "I don't want to see any rats."

"Pack rats are interesting animals," Rosie said. "They like shiny objects, but they don't just steal things; they often trade, leaving something to replace what they take."

"Rosie reads a lot," Kayo said.

"So do I," said Elisabeth. "But not about rats."

"Something ate part of this prickly pear," Kayo said. She pointed to several places where large bite marks were visible. Chunks of the cactus were missing, obviously eaten.

"I wonder if coyotes eat the prickly pears," Rosie said.

They leaned closer, examining the bite marks. When they stopped talking, they heard movement beneath a shrub. A small gray mouse darted out and ran to a clump of wildflowers. Soon another mouse appeared, and another. The girls stood still, watching and listening, as many mice scurried around in the dim light.

"I wonder if those are pack rats," Kayo whispered.

"Rats are bigger," Rosie said. "Pack rats are about eight inches long, not counting their tails."

The last bit of sun slipped beneath the horizon. "We'd better go back," Kayo said. "Your parents said to be home before dark."

"My mother gets hysterical if I'm late," Elisabeth said. She zipped her windbreaker. "Besides," she added, "I don't like being here after dark with rats and coyotes."

"Rats," said Rosie, "are most active at night."

Sometimes Kayo wished Rosie didn't read so much. She was not eager to meet rats in the desert at night.

The girls ran up the trail, with Kayo in the lead, Elisabeth next, and Rosie last. As they rounded a curve, some loose gravel flew up from Kayo's tennis shoe. When Elisabeth's foot landed on it, she slipped. Teetering sideways, she stuck out her hands to try to catch her balance.

Rosie, who was right behind Elisabeth, couldn't stop in time. She ran into Elisabeth, and Elisabeth crashed to the ground.

There was a sickening *crack* as she landed.

Rosie fell, too. She landed on her hands and knees, skidding along the path. The gravel scratched her palms and ripped the knees of her jeans.

Kayo turned and hurried back. "What happened?" she said.

Rosie stood and rubbed her hands together, wiping off the grit. "I'm sorry, Elisabeth," she said. "I didn't mean to run into you."

"It wasn't your fault. I slipped on some stones." Elisabeth's voice sounded hollow, as if she were speaking into a tin can.

"Are you okay?" Rosie asked. She held out her hand to help Elisabeth up but Elisabeth did not take it.

Instead, Elisabeth leaned sideways on one elbow, with one leg bent under her and the other sticking out in front. She rubbed her hand back and forth on the ankle of the bent leg.

"I think I broke my leg," the hollow voice said. "It hurts really bad when I try to move."

Rosie realized Elisabeth sounded strange because she was trying not to cry.

"Don't get up," Rosie said. "You might make it worse if you stand on it. Stay here and I'll go get my parents."

"If her leg is broken," Kayo said, "she needs

medics. There's a phone next to the community bulletin board."

"I'll call nine one one," Rosie said. "They'll send an ambulance."

"I'll wait here with Elisabeth," Kayo said.

"We have a telephone in the motor home," Elisabeth said.

"I'll go there, then," Rosie said. "It's closer and I should tell your parents, anyway." She hurried up the trail toward the campsites.

Kayo sat beside Elisabeth and patted her shoulder.

Silent tears slipped down Elisabeth's cheeks. "I hope my dad got home. My mother goes all to pieces when anything bad happens."

"We should have told Rosie to tell her parents, too. They could help."

"Go after her," Elisabeth said. "Have her tell them first, and they can go along to tell my mother. Mom was a basket case when I chipped a tooth. She'll really come unglued over this."

Kayo hesitated. "I don't like to leave you here alone."

"I'll be okay."

"Are you sure?"

"Yes." Elisabeth sniffed. "Hurry," she said.

Kayo took off as if she were trying to beat out a bunt. She caught up with Rosie at the point where the trail intersected the road through the campsites. Breathlessly, while they ran, she told Rosie what Elisabeth had said.

"You tell Elisabeth's mother and call the medics," Rosie said. "I'll get my parents and meet you at the Lynwoods' motor home."

"Right."

They ran together until the road branched. Then Kayo ran to the left, toward the Lynwoods' big silver motor home, and Rosie ran to the right, toward her own motor home.

Rosie was out of breath by the time she got there. "Mom!" she called as she ran up the entry of her campsite. "Dad! We need help!"

Inside the motor home Bone Breath barked wildly.

Rosie grabbed the door handle and yanked. It did not open. The door was locked; her parents were gone.

Rosie saw a note taped on the top of the door.

Rosie and Kayo: We are out looking for you. If you get home before we're back, STAY HERE AND WAIT FOR US. We don't want you wandering around after dark.

Rosie could tell from the tone of the note that her mom had been annoyed when she wrote it.

We should have come back earlier, Rosie thought. We should not have made them worry about us.

Well, it was too late now. And she couldn't stay here and wait for them to return, either. If Elisabeth's mother got hysterical, Kayo would need Rosie to help calm Mrs. Lynwood down. And someone had to get back to Elisabeth.

Rosie took the pencil from her vocabulary notebook and scribbled on the bottom of her parents' note to her: *Our new friend broke her leg, and we are helping her. We are okay.*

If her parents came back, they wouldn't worry any longer, and they wouldn't keep looking for Rosie and Kayo. They would know there was a good reason why Rosie and Kayo were so late.

Rosie ran toward the Lynwoods' motor home. Maybe, with luck, her parents were looking for her in that part of the campground and she would find them before she caught up with Kayo. She hoped so. It would be easier to deal with this problem if Mom and Dad were there to help.

She did not find her parents.

Chapter

*G*et ready," Jasper whispered.

At the picnic table next to the red pickup, Benny dropped his cards.

"She's coming," Jasper said. "And she's alone."

Benny stared through the dim light. Jasper was right. A girl about twelve years old, with long blond hair, was running down the road toward the silver motor home. She was tall and thin, just like Jasper had said the Lynwood kid was.

Jasper watched the girl for a few seconds longer. "Let's go!" he said. "Start the truck."

Benny bolted away from the picnic table the way a racehorse leaves the starting gate. He plucked the truck keys out of his pocket with one hand as he ran. He opened the door of the truck, climbed in, and started the engine.

Jasper walked quietly away from the picnic table toward the road. He reached the silver motor home's site a few moments before the girl got there.

Kayo didn't notice him. She was running hard, and when she reached the entrance to the Lynwoods' campsite, she cut the corner and headed for their motor home.

Jasper moved fast. In two steps he was behind her. He grabbed her shoulder with one hand, and at the same time he clamped the other hand over her mouth so she couldn't scream.

Behind him, he heard the pickup approaching. Good job, Benny, he thought. Your timing is perfect. And Benny remembered not to turn the lights on yet. They didn't want to advertise what they were doing, for all the world to see.

Benny pulled the pickup part way into the Lynwoods' campsite.

Kayo kicked and struggled. In the tussle the man's arm brushed her Kansas City Royals baseball cap from her head. It fell to the ground.

"Don't make it hard on yourself," he muttered as he dragged her toward the pickup.

Benny pulled on the parking brake but left the motor running. He jumped out, grabbed the rope and the gag from the front seat, and went to help

Jasper. Quickly they stuffed the gag into Kayo's mouth so she couldn't yell.

Benny held Kayo's arms behind her back while Jasper tied her wrists together. Kayo twisted and turned, trying to get away, but the men were much stronger than she was.

They bound her ankles together next, winding the rope tightly around them. Then Jasper wound the last of the rope around her waist, binding her arms to her sides.

They stood at the rear of the pickup. Exhaust fumes from the idling motor filled Kayo's nose when she inhaled. I'm going to be sick, she thought, as panic and nausea rose in the back of her throat.

Jasper reached for the door on the back end of the pickup. "Benny!" he said. "You forgot to unlock the door."

Benny bolted back to the cab of the pickup, turned off the engine, and removed the key. Jasper kept his hands firmly on Kayo's shoulders; she could feel his fingers through her shirt.

Rosie ran toward the camping loop where the silver motor home was parked. She kept her head down as she ran, watching the dark pavement. She didn't want to fall, as Elisabeth had.

When she rounded the corner where she knew she would be able to see the Lynwoods' motor home, she looked up. Another vehicle was parked directly in front of the Lynwoods' campsite. Elisabeth had said her father towed a small sports car, but this vehicle was larger than that.

Rosie had a pain in her side from running. She slowed, straining her eyes to see as she walked closer. It was a pickup truck with a camper on the back. Were they planning to drive Elisabeth to the hospital in someone's camper? Curious, she hurried forward.

Benny thrust a key in the lock on the camper door. Leaving the keys dangling, he turned the handle and opened the door.

Kayo knew they were going to put her inside and drive her away. But where? Why? Who were these men? And what did they want with her? She tried to scream, but the sound, muffled by the gag in her mouth, was barely audible even to herself.

Kayo felt helpless and scared. Where is everyone? she wondered. Why doesn't someone come along, walking a dog or jogging or heading for the rest rooms?

One person. That's all it would take. If just one person saw what was happening, surely that person would summon help. But if nobody saw her now, it would be too late. Once she was put in the camper and driven away, her chances of being rescued would drop like a sinker ball crossing the plate.

"Let's get out of here," Jasper said, "before the kid's mother comes back."

Rosie stopped walking. She blinked at the scene ahead of her as prickles of fear rose on her arms and crept up the back of her neck. Those men had Kayo tied up!

One of them bent down, put an arm behind Kayo's knees, and lifted her in his arms.

"Hey!" Rosie yelled. "What's going on here?"

He set Kayo back on her feet and stood in front of her.

Kayo couldn't see around him, but she recognized the voice, and her fear eased. Rosie and her parents were here. They would rescue her.

"Jasper!" Benny said. "It's another kid."

Only a kid? Kayo thought. What about Mr. and Mrs. Saunders? Rosie had gone to get her parents; where were they? And where was Elisabeth's mother? Mrs. Lynwood must hear their voices. Why didn't she come out of her motor home to see what was happening in her campsite?

Kayo leaned against the camper to steady herself, still hoping Mr. and Mrs. Saunders would appear behind Rosie.

"She sees what we're doing," Benny said.

"Take care of her," Jasper said.

Benny bolted away from the camper toward Rosie.

Jasper picked Kayo up again. This time he dumped her into the camper. "Big money, here we come," he said.

Kayo landed on her side, clunking her arm on the hard floor. A bolt of pain shot through her elbow.

He slammed the door.

Run, Rosie, Kayo thought. Get help!

When Rosie saw the big man run toward her, she realized it had been a mistake to yell. She should have gone for help, before the men saw her. She spun around and dashed back the way she had come.

Rosie saw lights in a small camper-van ahead. "Help!" she called.

The word was smothered by an arm that came around her head from behind. The man yanked back, holding Rosie's neck in the crook of his elbow and forcing her head backward. He clapped the other hand over her mouth and growled in her ear, "Don't make a sound or you'll never speak again." Then he turned her around and shoved her toward the pickup.

Terrified, Rosie kept quiet.

Chapter

Click. From inside the camper Kayo heard the sound of the door locking. Scream, Rosie, she thought. Get help for us before it's too late.

Rosie watched the big man open the door on the passenger side of the pickup. "Get in," he said, letting go of Rosie's head, "and keep still."

Rosie got in the truck. I have to make noise, she thought. I have to get other people to notice us. If no one sees us, they'll drive us out of here and nobody will know where to find us. She could almost see the headlines of the morning newspaper: TWO GIRLS VANISH FROM CAMPGROUND.

"Slide over in the middle," the man said, "and make room for me." Rosie slid, but instead of sitting silently while he got in beside her, she reached over to the steering wheel and honked the horn.

Honk! Honk! Honk-honk-honk!

That should attract some attention, Rosie thought as she thumped the horn over and over.

The man cursed and dived into the pickup, jerking Rosie's hands away from the horn.

At the same time the second man opened the driver's door and got in behind the wheel. "Benny!" he said as he fumbled to put the key in the ignition. "Keep her quiet."

The outdoor light on the camper across the road came on.

The second man started the engine. "Trade places with her," he said, "so she can't reach the horn."

The big man climbed over Rosie and sat in the middle, shoving her toward the door. "Do that again," he said, "and you'll need plastic surgery on your nose. Right, Jasper?"

Jasper switched on the headlights and drove toward the campground exit.

The names Benny and Jasper meant nothing to Rosie. "Who are you?" she asked. "Where are you taking us?"

The men ignored her questions.

"You dimwit," Jasper said. "I told you to take care of her."

"I did take care of her. She's here, isn't she?"

"Yes, she's here. I meant, scare her off, not

44

bring her along. What are we going to do with her now?"

"Tell Lynwood he gets two for the price of one."

"Oh, sure," the driver said. "He doesn't want an extra kid."

"How do you know? Elisabeth's friend probably has money to burn. Maybe there'll be two ransoms. Maybe we'll get paid double."

Rosie's mouth was dry. Ransom! Who were these men and how did they know that she was Elisabeth's friend? She and Kayo had only known Elisabeth a few hours.

"Fat chance of getting double the money," Jasper said. "What makes you think this one's worth anything?"

"People like the Lynwoods don't pal around with bums."

Jasper tapped his fingers on the steering wheel. "Maybe you're right. If they brought her along, her parents probably own two-thirds of Microsoft or Ford Motor."

"We'll get paid for the one in back and paid again for this one."

Rosie frowned. The men talked as if they expected to get a ransom for Kayo. What a joke. Kayo's mom could barely afford to pay the rent and buy groceries. She would never be able to raise any money for a ransom. So, why would anyone kidnap Kayo? And why were they talking about Elisabeth's parents?

The answer, when Rosie thought of it, was so obvious she wondered why she didn't catch on right away. Elisabeth's parents must be wealthy. They did have a huge motor home. And Elisabeth had traveled all over the world.

"You took the wrong girl," Rosie said.

"Quiet!" Benny said, and he clamped his hand across Rosie's mouth.

"Wait a minute," Jasper said. "Let her talk."

The hand was removed.

"You're after Elisabeth Lynwood, aren't you?" Rosie said. "You knew the Lynwoods were staying here and you saw Kayo running toward their motor home and you thought it was Elisabeth. They *do* kind of look alike, with their blond hair. And they're the same age. But it isn't Elisabeth that you tied up and put in the camper. It's Kayo Benton and her mom doesn't have an extra dime to give you for a ransom."

"Nice try, kid," Jasper said. "I admire your creativity, making up a story like that on the spur of the moment."

"It isn't a story," Rosie insisted. "You won't get any ransom for Kayo or for me, either, so you may as well let us go." Rosie's parents, unlike

Kayo's mother, had ample income, but Rosie saw no reason to say so. Let them think she was penniless.

"I don't believe you," Jasper said. "That can't be the wrong girl."

"It is," Rosie said. "Elisabeth Lynwood was with us, but that isn't who you tied up. The girl you put in the camper is Kayo Benton."

"No," Jasper said.

"What if she's right?" Benny asked. "What'll we do then?"

"If we have the wrong girl," Jasper said, "the whole deal is off. There's no way to go back now and get the right one, not until we get rid of these two. By then, their families will have cops crawling over the campground like ants on an anthill."

"How do we find out?" Benny said. "The kid wasn't carrying a purse or anything. There's no identification. How do we know for sure who it is?"

There was an edge of panic in his voice. He didn't like what Jasper was saying, not one little bit.

The pickup was almost to the park entry station, where people paid their fees and registered to stay at the campground. This, Rosie thought, would be her best chance to get help. When the pickup passed the building, she would scream for help. Even with the pickup windows shut, some-one might hear her.

She tensed, waiting for the right moment.

"Get her head down," Jasper said, "in case someone's on duty."

Benny's hand hit the back of Rosie's head and shoved it toward her knees. He leaned forward, shielding her from the view of anyone looking in the window.

Mr. Harris, the campground host, sat in the entry station, reading a book.

"Help!" Rosie yelled, but with her head pressed into her knees, the sound was muffled by her own pant legs.

Mr. Harris glanced up as the pickup passed. Jasper waved at him. Mr. Harris waved back.

"We're out of here," Jasper said as the pickup drove on.

Benny took his hand off Rosie's head.

They rode along in silence for several minutes.

"If you let me and Kayo go now," Rosie said, "you could probably get away before the police come."

"The police are not coming," Jasper said.

"Oh, yes, they are. My parents will report us missing when we don't go back to our motor home."

"As soon as Jasper makes his phone call," Benny said, "they'll know *why* you didn't come home."

"His phone call?"

"To Andrew Lynwood. Your friend's daddy."

"My parents have never met Andrew Lynwood," Rosie said. "A phone call to him won't keep my parents from calling the police."

"Shut up," said Jasper. "Both of you."

"You have the wrong girl," Rosie repeated.

"She's lying," Jasper said. "She has to be. The girl we got matches Elisabeth's description perfectly, and she was running straight for the Lynwood motor home."

"The girl you tied up is Kayo, and she was running to tell Mr. and Mrs. Lynwood that Elisabeth fell and broke her leg."

"I think she's telling the truth," Benny said. "How could she make up a broken leg so fast?" His voice rose to a whine. "It's true, Jasper. We got the wrong kid."

Jasper swore.

"What are we going to do, Jasper?"

"If we do not have Elisabeth Lynwood in the back of this camper," Jasper said slowly, "we will have two bodies to dispose of."

Horror shot through Rosie, making her heart

pound. She knew the two bodies he meant would be her and Kayo.

They rode in silence for a time. Rosie watched the dark desert through the window. It would be safer, she decided, to let them think that Kayo was Elisabeth. If the men believed they could collect a big ransom for Kayo, and for her, they would keep the girls safe.

"You won't be able to call my parents to ask for a ransom," Rosie said. "They're in France. That's why the Lynwoods brought me along."

"Ha!" said Jasper. "You *are* Elisabeth's buddy and we do have the right kid."

Rosie put her hand over her mouth, as if she had just realized she'd made a mistake and admitted who she really was.

Rosie slowly lowered her hand. "I lied to you before," she said. "You do have Elisabeth tied up. And my parents are the Lynwoods' best friends. My dad is Mr. Lynwood's assistant."

"I knew it," Jasper said. "I don't make mistakes when there's this much money involved."

Benny glared at Rosie. First she showed up at the last second and spoiled their perfect plan, and then she scared him with her lies about taking the wrong girl. He had half a mind to teach this kid a lesson she wouldn't forget. He didn't like her. He didn't like her one bit.

Rosie saw the anger in Benny's eyes. I have to get away, she thought. Something terrible is going to happen if I don't. As soon as they make the ransom call, they'll discover the truth, and then what will they do?

Kayo was tied up in the back of the camper. Elisabeth was lying alone in the dark with a broken leg. Rosie was the only one who could save them—and save herself. She closed her eyes and tried to think how she could escape.

I'll jump out of the truck, she decided.

She looked out the window. They were still passing desert. She leaned slightly to her left until she could read the speedometer. He was driving thirty miles an hour. Rosie wondered how bad the impact would be if she jumped from a truck going thirty miles an hour.

She swallowed hard, trying to work up the courage. She knew if she jumped, she might injure herself badly. But if she didn't jump, what would happen to her?

And what about Kayo? Rosie knew Elisabeth would be found eventually; her life was not in danger. But Kayo's life was, and no one except Rosie knew where to look for Kayo.

She had to jump. It was her only chance to escape.

Do it now, she told herself, before he gets to a freeway and picks up speed.

Her right hand crept forward and found the door handle. Not giving herself time to change her mind, she jerked it back. The door flew open. Rosie clenched her teeth and rolled sideways out of the moving truck.

In the instant before she hit the pavement, she remembered the terrible cracking sound that Elisabeth's leg had made when the bone snapped.

Chapter

*Y*ou dimwit!" Jasper exploded. "You let her get away!"

Benny braced his feet on the floor and gripped the dashboard with his left hand while he leaned out and grabbed the door handle. He slammed the door shut.

"How *could* you?" Jasper yelled. "She heard everything we said. She knows the plan. She knows what we look like."

Sweat dripped down the back of Benny's neck. His heart drummed in his chest. He was furious—at himself for not hanging on to the girl, at the girl for making him look stupid, and at Jasper for yelling at him. He could feel his face flushing, the way it always did when he was angry.

"Good riddance," Benny said. "I hope she killed herself."

"If she didn't," Jasper said, "she'll run to the nearest telephone and call the cops and give them a description of us and the truck." He stomped his foot on the brake. "Why didn't you hold on to her?" he said.

"How did I know she'd be fool enough to jump out of a moving truck?"

"We'll have to go back," Jasper said as the truck screeched to a stop. "We can't take a chance that she's able to walk."

In the back of the camper Kayo rolled from side to side, unable to brace herself. I have to get loose, she thought. I have to get out of here before we get wherever it is we are going. But how? When she tried to move her hands, the rope cut into her wrists.

She wondered whether Rosie had been able to get help. She had heard Rosie yell; she knew Rosie saw her tied up. But Rosie couldn't run as fast as Kayo could. Had she been able to get away? Had she called the police by now—or was Rosie tied up somewhere, too?

When her eyes adjusted to the faint light, Kayo looked around the interior of the small camper. There were wooden benches on both sides, with a window over each bench. Faded green curtains, with a fishing pole print, covered the windows. There was no camping equipment, no clothing, no ice chest or tackle box—none of the gear that you would expect in a camper. It was as if the men never planned to stay in it overnight.

The truck went over a speed bump, and Kayo bounced helplessly. Her thoughts whirled around like a spinning jump rope. If the men had abducted Rosie, too, they would have thrown her in the camper with me. Or maybe not. If they didn't have more rope to tie Rosie with, they wouldn't put her back here because if her hands were free, she could untie me. Maybe Rosie was up in front, in the truck with the men. Maybe that's who had honked the horn.

Well, it didn't do any good to worry about Rosie. And she couldn't count on Rosie bringing help, either. She would have to do something to save herself.

If I could stand up, Kayo thought, or get up on one of those benches, I could stick my head under the curtain and bang my head on the window when we pass anyone. Maybe someone would see me and realize I need help.

She lay on her back and wriggled sideways until she was flush against one of the benches. Then she sat up and turned, so her back was against the bench. She bent her knees, braced her back against the bench, and tried to stand. It didn't work.

Next she rolled sideways and got up on her knees. She leaned forward, resting her chest on one of the wooden benches. The truck hit a pothole; Kayo bounced, hitting her chin hard on the bench. She raised her ankles and pressed the toes of her tennis shoes into the floor, pushing herself up. Gradually she worked her way onto the bench.

She sat up next to the window and put her head under the curtain. It smelled musty. Kayo sneezed. She looked out into the darkness. She wasn't positive, but she thought the pickup was going down the road that Mr. Saunders had used when they drove to Usery Mountain Recreation Area. If so, Kayo knew they were headed south, toward the freeway.

There were no houses, only empty fields. Too late, Kayo realized she should have climbed on the other bench, where anyone driving in the opposite direction might see her.

As Kayo gazed at the darkness along the side of the road, a person flashed through her line of vision. The body came and went, falling from the front of the truck to the pavement before she could focus on it. She pressed her head to the window, trying to see.

Kayo got only a glimpse of the person, but it was enough. She saw a flash of purple T-shirt and knew it was Rosie. The men must have pushed Rosie out of the truck.

Kayo fought back tears. Rosie was lying back there in the road with no way to get help. She might have broken bones. She might have a skull fracture. She might . . . Kayo pushed the next thought out of her mind. It was too terrible even to consider.

The pickup jerked and Kayo heard the squeal of the brakes. Seconds later the truck swung in a circle. Unable to hold on to anything to steady herself, Kayo toppled off the bench and hit her head on the floor.

She lay still. Every inch of her body ached from the jolt. Those men, she thought, are dangerous, and I am completely helpless. She could hold back her tears no longer.

Rosie landed in the gravel on the shoulder of the road and rolled into the drainage ditch. She heard the tires squeal as the pickup braked to a stop.

She sat up, quickly flexing her arms and legs. Her elbow was scraped and bleeding, and she knew she'd be covered with bruises tomorrow, but nothing seemed to be broken.

I have to run, she thought. If the truck is stopping, it means they're coming back for me.

She scrambled to her feet and looked up and down the road, hoping she might flag down a passing car and get help. She saw only the red taillights and brake lights of the pickup. There were no other cars.

The brake lights went off. The pickup made a U-turn and headed back toward Rosie.

The headlights clicked from dim to bright, illuminating a wide arc of pavement.

I can't stay on the road, Rosie thought, or in the ditch, either. They'll see me, and they can go faster than I can; I'd never get away.

My only chance is to hide.

Rosie climbed out the far side of the ditch and ran into the desert. Ahead, she saw a large chain fruit cholla. It was twice Rosie's height and four feet wide, with thick branches twisted together like a braided rug.

She ran to the cholla and hid behind it, being careful not to lean close enough to get stuck. Moving slightly as the truck approached, she kept the cactus between herself and the pickup, blocking the men's view.

The truck moved slowly. Rosie held her breath

as it passed her hiding place and continued down the road. The truck went a hundred feet beyond the point where Rosie had leaped out.

"Stop!" Benny said. "You're going too far. The kid jumped out way back there."

The truck stopped. "We'll find her," Benny said. "Don't worry, Jasper. If she's alive, she's probably banged up and won't be able to walk. We'll find her."

As he talked, he slid out of the truck and slammed the door behind him. He crossed the road and ran along the shoulder, back toward the spot where he was sure the kid had jumped.

He expected Jasper to come, too. He expected to hear Jasper's door slam shut and Jasper's footsteps hurrying across the road to help Benny search. Instead, he heard the engine accelerate.

The red pickup made another U-turn and headed south again, the way they were going when the girl jumped. It passed Benny and sped off down the road toward town.

Benny's mouth hung open. He stared at the taillights until they disappeared in the distance, tiny pinpoints of red fading to nothing.

Jasper had left him. Left him! He was in the middle of nowhere with no money and no transportation while Jasper was speeding back to town to collect the ransom.

He'll keep my share, Benny thought. That stinking double-crosser will keep my five thousand dollars.

It was all the second girl's fault. If she had not arrived when she did, none of this would have happened. The whole deal had been smooth as syrup, until she showed up. Because of her, Benny was standing here alone on the side of the road, while Jasper made off with the money.

His anger focused on the girl. Like an enraged bull, Benny charged forward. He would find that girl if he had to hunt all night. Find her and make her sorry for cheating him out of his money.

Chapter

Elisabeth heard rustling noises in the dark. She lay still, listening. What if it was a rat? What if it was several rats? She shuddered. She was lying only a short distance from the pack rat's nest, and Rosie had said they were active at night.

She wondered what kind of animal had eaten the tops of the prickly pear cactus. Something big enough to have a large set of teeth.

What was taking Rosie and Kayo so long? They should be back by now, with her mom and Rosie's parents.

Across the black desert a coyote yipped. Other coyotes joined the chorus. She thought coyotes were beautiful animals. Ordinarily, she would be thrilled to hear their cries; but the wild sound made her skin crawl now that she was lying alone and unable to walk.

Something's wrong, Elisabeth decided. Kayo and Rosie would not run off and leave her alone for such a long time unless something had happened to them. But what could have happened?

She heard the rustling noise again. What if the rats came over to her? What if they crawled on her? What if one of them bit her? Her stomach turned somersaults.

Stop it, she told herself. Don't get hysterical, like Mom does.

Elisabeth's mother always worked herself into a froth over every little problem, waving her hands dramatically as she reported her imaginary fears. Elisabeth hated it when Mom did that, and now here she was, doing the same thing.

I'll hum, she decided. Grandma used to tell me to hum when I didn't want to go to bed because I was scared of the shadows. "Hum, Elisabeth," Grandma instructed. "Music chases all the goblins away." And so three-year-old Elisabeth lay in bed humming "Twinkle, Twinkle, Little Star" until she fell asleep.

Now, with her leg throbbing, she lay in the dark desert and tried to hum, but despite the twinkling stars overhead, her mouth was so full of fear and pain, she couldn't make the sound come out.

She closed her eyes and took a deep breath, willing the pain to go away. The rustling grew louder. And closer.

I have to get up, Elisabeth thought. No matter how much my leg hurts, I can't lie here any longer or I'll go crazy. If I can get myself upright, maybe I can hop back to camp on one leg.

She bent her good leg and rolled facedown, easing her weight onto her knees. She put her left foot on the ground, and pushing with her hands, she got up, balancing on the left leg. When she stood, however, the blood rushed downward, making her broken right leg throb even more.

Elisabeth cried out. She felt faint. Swaying dizzily, she tried to hop forward. Instead, she fell again, crumpling in a heap on the path.

The pain in her leg was worse now.

The coyotes howled again. The sound was louder. Closer.

Elisabeth put her head on the ground and sobbed.

Mr. and Mrs. Saunders peered anxiously out the window at the silent campground. "This is not like Rosie," Mrs. Saunders said. "It's nearly ten o'clock." She petted the kitten, who was curled in her lap. The kitten stretched out her front paws and purred.

"If her new friend broke her leg," Mr. Saunders said, "why haven't we heard an ambulance? Rosie knows enough to call an ambulance."

"Let's walk around the camp one more time," Mrs. Saunders said. She put Phoenix on the sofa. Bone Breath immediately jumped up next to Phoenix and tried to lick her face. Phoenix batted at him. "We can take Bone Breath, too, so we won't have to walk him again before we go to bed." She put a small plastic bag in her pocket, in case she needed to clean up after Bone Breath.

At the sight of the leash Bone Breath leaped to the floor, slobbering and wagging with delight. The sudden movement startled Phoenix, who hissed and climbed up the curtain.

"The next time we want a relaxing vacation," Mr. Saunders said, "we'll fly somewhere, just the two of us, and stay in a hotel." He knew he sounded crabby, but he couldn't help it. He read the newspapers and watched the television news; he knew the terrible things that can happen to young girls. *Where were they?*

Mr. and Mrs. Saunders started down the road again, pausing often while Bone Breath sniffed at bushes.

A small black convertible drove slowly past

them, with its top down. Mr. Saunders let out a low whistle. "That's a 1955 Thunderbird," he said softly. "A true classic."

The car pulled into a campsite with a huge silver motor home. A man got out. Immediately the door of the motor home flew open and a woman stepped out. "Thank goodness you're home!" she cried. Her voice was high and shrill, as if she were fighting for control. "Elisabeth has disappeared."

Mr. and Mrs. Saunders stopped abruptly. They looked at each other and then rushed toward the other people.

"When?" cried the man. "What happened?"

"She left me a note about a kitten and some new friends named Kayo and Rosie, and she said she'd be home before dark, but she never came. Oh, Andrew, I'm so worried! Something has happened to her. I can feel it in my bones."

Mr. and Mrs. Saunders ran to the other couple.

"We're Rosie's parents," Mrs. Saunders said. "She and Kayo are not back, either."

For an instant everyone talked at once, trying to figure out what had happened.

When Mrs. Lynwood heard about Rosie's note, she started to cry. "Oh, no," she sobbed, sounding more hysterical by the second. "Where is she? My baby is lying alone somewhere, in pain."

Mr. Lynwood went in the motor home and picked up a cellular telephone. As he came back out, he spoke into it. "We need police and an ambulance in the Usery Mountain Recreation Area. Three young girls are missing, and we think one of them has a broken leg. Please hurry."

Mrs. Saunders gave him an approving look. She liked people who knew how to respond to an emergency.

"I'll alert the campground hosts," Mr. Saunders said. "Then I'll wait at the entry station for the police and the ambulance."

He held the flashlight toward his wife. "Here," he said. "You take this."

"You keep it," Mrs. Saunders said. "You can look for the girls while you wait for the police. I'll take Bone Breath home and get the other flashlight and meet you at the entry station."

"Oh, poor Elisabeth," Mrs. Lynwood said. "Where is my girl?"

When Mr. Saunders turned to leave, the light from the flashlight hit something on the ground. He bent to pick it up, then turned to his wife. "It's Kayo's baseball cap," he said.

"Are you sure it's hers?" Mrs. Saunders said.

"She was wearing her Royals cap today. I kidded her about it, said she had better not wear that one tomorrow when we watch the Giants and the Mariners."

"Kayo would not leave one of her hats behind," Mrs. Saunders said. "Not by choice."

"Maybe she had no choice," Mr. Saunders said.

Mrs. Lynwood sobbed Elisabeth's name, over and over.

Mr. Saunders took off toward the hosts' site, running hard. Mrs. Saunders and Bone Breath hurried away, too.

Mr. Lynwood put his arm around his wife's shoulder and steered her toward the door of their motor home.

Mrs. Lynwood sobbed louder. "Something terrible has happened to my baby!" she cried.

Chapter

*R*osie crouched behind the big cholla.

Peeking out, she watched the pickup pass her and speed toward town. A sense of relief poured over her like hot fudge over ice cream, melting the cold ball of fear in her stomach. They were gone. They had left her behind.

The relief lasted only a second. The men still had Kayo, tied up in the back of the camper.

The ball of fear returned, only this time she feared for her friend, rather than for herself.

Rosie shrugged her shoulders, flexing her sore arms. She could almost feel her elbows turning black and blue. She moved away from the huge cholla, being careful not to step on any of the clumps that had fallen from it to the ground.

She was sore and tired, but she would walk

back to Usery Mountain Recreation Area. It couldn't be more than a mile or two; she had not been in the truck very long.

A crescent moon stood on end like a shallow bowl, spilling a dim light. Rosie walked across the desert toward the road. She was almost to the pavement when she heard the footsteps.

Thump. Thump. Thump.

Someone was coming.

Rosie's head jerked up; she looked toward the sound.

The big man—Benny—was not speeding toward town in the pickup truck with his partner, as she had thought. He was running along the side of the road, toward her.

For an instant Rosie froze, staring at him. She could tell when he saw her. His arm came up and his finger pointed at her. Then he began to run faster.

Rosie scrambled back across the ditch and took off through the desert. He would catch her for sure if she stayed on the road. The chances of getting help from a passing motorist seemed remote. She had not seen a single vehicle pass since she jumped from the truck.

"You can't get away!" he yelled.

I need a weapon, Rosie thought. If I could find a rock, maybe I could throw it at him and knock him out. But she saw no rocks big enough, and she decided that wouldn't work, anyway. She wasn't like Kayo, who practiced pitching all the time. Rosie's aim was poor. Even if she did find a rock, she'd probably miss the man.

She dodged around the cactus she had hidden behind. I wish he'd run into a chain fruit cholla, she thought. That would slow him down.

He was closer now. Glancing over her shoulder, Rosie saw the dark form, his arms out, reaching for her. And if he caught her? What then?

Rosie looked forward again just in time. She had almost collided with a cholla herself. Pieces of it littered the ground; Rosie's foot came down on one of the spiny segments.

Her foot slipped out from under her and she nearly fell. As she struggled to keep her balance, she realized she had discovered her weapon, if she had some way to pick it up.

Rosie reached into her back pocket and pulled out the pencil that she always carried with her vocabulary notebook. Quickly she squatted beside the fallen pieces of cholla. Grasping the pencil in her fist, she jabbed the pointed end as hard as she could into the largest piece of cactus, a section as big as a saucer.

She held the pencil up, with the piece of cactus stuck on the end of it like a giant prickly lollipop.

She stood up again just as Benny caught up with her.

She kept the hand that held the cactus behind her, being careful to hold it well away from her back.

For one split second she looked directly into his eyes and saw hatred and anger simmering there.

At that moment Rosie heard a siren. Benny's head turned toward the sound. Rosie stepped away from him and looked at the road. Whirling red lights rushed forward out of the darkness. The siren grew louder.

Rosie gripped the pencil and, using all her strength, swung her arm toward him.

Benny reacted instantly. His hand went up, shoulder high, but he was a fraction of a second too late. As his fist swung toward Rosie's head, she jabbed the cactus in his face, hitting his cheek just below his left eye.

She let go of the pencil. The cactus stuck to his face.

The siren wailed louder.

Benny swore and tried to shove the cactus off. Instead, he only pushed it deeper into his cheek. Spines stuck in the palm of his hand. He bellowed with rage and pain.

Rosie bolted toward the road. The siren and

the flashing lights were almost there. "Help!" she screamed. "Help me!"

Lights outlined the white vehicle; she saw a red stripe on its side. Rosie waved her arms over her head as she ran. "Over here!" she shouted, but the siren drowned out her words.

She was still in the field, among the cacti, when the ambulance roared past. Whoever was in it had not seen her.

Tears stung Rosie's eyes but she kept running. She hoped the ambulance was on the way to help Elisabeth.

Down the ditch she skidded, and up the other side to the road. Her tennis shoes pounded on the black pavement, running after the ambulance, running from the man, running back to camp.

She didn't dare slow down. She knew Benny would chase her again the second he got all the spines out of this face. Maybe sooner. He had been angry before; she didn't want to think how he would be now that she had jabbed him in the face with a cactus.

Mrs. Saunders hurried anxiously toward her motor home, with Bone Breath trotting beside her. How could three twelve-year-old girls disappear into thin air?

Bone Breath stopped so suddenly that Mrs. Saunders nearly tripped over him. "Come on," she said, tugging the leash.

The terrier refused to budge.

"You can't chase a rabbit now," she said, pulling harder.

Bone Breath strained in the other direction. Mrs. Saunders realized he was trying to go down a narrow path that branched off the main road. She had not noticed the path earlier.

She stepped back to where Bone Breath stood and saw a small wooden sign. She bent down, trying to read it in the faint moonlight. NATURE TRAIL. At dinner Rosie and Kayo talked about a trail where they were learning the names of the plants for their vocabulary game.

Bone Breath tugged harder, pulling her away from the paved road. Mrs. Saunders hesitated about going off onto a trail without telling anyone. There were too many missing persons in this camp already.

On the other hand, she knew dogs have a better sense of smell than humans do. Was it possible that Bone Breath had picked up Rosie's scent on this trail? Was Bone Breath trying to lead her to the girls?

"All right," she said, wishing she had kept the flashlight. "Let's go."

Bone Breath bounded forward along the trail. Mrs. Saunders followed, hoping she wasn't making a mistake.

When they rounded a curve, Bone Breath tugged harder, trying to go faster.

From ahead in the darkness Mrs. Saunders heard a faint sound.

Bone Breath heard it, too. He lunged forward, jerking the leash out of her hand.

Benny picked the spines from his face as he ran. His cheek burned, his eye was watering, and the spines pricked his fingers when he tried to grasp them to pull them out. He pressed his throbbing palm to his mouth and tasted blood.

Fueled by anger and pain, he ran after Rosie. She had a good head start, but he would find her, if it was the last thing he ever did.

Headlights came from behind in the right lane. Benny's shadow, long and dark, ran down the road ahead of him. Benny, on the left side of the road, didn't look around or stop running. He would catch the girl first and hitch a ride later.

When the car went past, Benny kept his eyes straight ahead, looking for the girl. She would stay on the road now, he was sure. And he would find her.

Farther up the road Rosie also saw the approaching headlights. She ran to the center of the road, waving her hands.

She knew she was taking a chance by flagging down a stranger. The person in the car could be a crazed maniac, for all she knew, but what did she have to lose? There was a crazed maniac running after her already. She had to gamble that the person in the car would be normal and willing to help her.

"Stop!" she called. "Stop! I need help!"

The lights came closer. Rosie closed her eyes against the brightness, waving frantically.

As she heard the vehicle slow, it dawned on her that the red pickup may have come back. She might be flagging down Kayo's kidnapper.

Chapter 10

*E*lisabeth tried not to faint. Feeling woozy from the pain, she closed her eyes and took deep breaths.

Everything seemed hazy as she drifted downward into unconsciousness.

She was roused from her stupor when something warm and wet brushed her hand. Her eyes flew open. She moved her hand and felt fur.

Elisabeth screamed.

Bone Breath barked.

"Rosie?" Mrs. Saunders said as she hurried forward. "Is that you?"

"Help!" Elisabeth said. "I'm here, on the ground."

Mrs. Saunders knelt and put her hand on Elisabeth's shoulder. "I'm Rosie's mother," she said.

Elisabeth burst into tears of relief.

"Your father has already called an ambulance," Mrs. Saunders said. "It will be here soon."

Elisabeth couldn't stop crying.

Bone Breath stood beside her, licking her hand.

"Do you know where Rosie and Kayo are?" Mrs. Saunders asked as she grabbed Bone Breath's leash.

Elisabeth shook her head. "No," she said. "They went to get you and my mother, but that was a long time ago. I don't know for sure how long; it seems like hours."

Mrs. Saunders took a tissue out of her pocket and gave it to Elisabeth. After Elisabeth blew her nose, she told Mrs. Saunders how she had fallen and the other girls left to get help. "They never came back," she said.

"I'll need to leave you for a few minutes, too," Mrs. Saunders said. "Just long enough to tell my husband where you are so he can direct the ambulance here as soon as it arrives."

A small groan escaped Elisabeth's lips at the idea of being left alone on the trail again, but she knew it had to be done.

"I'll tell your parents where you are, too," Mrs. Saunders added.

"Mom's probably throwing a fit," Elisabeth said.

Mrs. Saunders refrained from saying, yes, she is. Instead she said, "Your mother is understandably worried about you."

And I am worried about Rosie and Kayo, Mrs. Saunders thought as she hurried back to the main road through camp. She ran to her own motor home, put Bone Breath inside with Phoenix, grabbed the extra flashlight, and started toward the entry gate. Before she got there, she saw the ambulance approaching.

Mrs. Saunders swung her flashlight back and forth, signaling the ambulance to come toward her. When it pulled alongside her, she cried, "Follow me!" and ran to where the nature trail branched off.

While the medics hurried down the trail toward Elisabeth, Mrs. Saunders went to the big silver motor home and told the Lynwoods where their daughter was.

But what about my daughter? she wondered. Where was Rosie? And Kayo, who seemed like a second daughter—where was she?

Rosie stood in the middle of the road, waving her arms as if she held signal flags. The car braked and pulled alongside her.

Rosie opened her eyes. It was a police car; a uniformed officer got out.

"There's a man chasing me!" she cried, pointing down the road. "Back there! He's after me!"

"Get in," the officer said, indicating the door on the passenger side of the patrol car.

While Rosie hurried around the front of the car and climbed in, he called for a backup unit.

"What's your name?" he asked.

When Rosie told him, he immediately made another call to say that she was with him. "Your family reported you and a friend missing," he said. "That's where I was going."

"My friend got kidnapped. They tried to take me, too, but I got away."

He turned off the car lights and stayed outside the car, with the door open, watching the road as Rosie told him everything that had happened.

"Did you get a license plate number on the truck?" he asked. He kept watching the road.

"No. Everything happened so fast. It was red, though. A red pickup, and the camper part was dark colored. Black, I think, or maybe dark brown."

The officer reported the events and description of the truck on his radio.

"Anything else?" he asked. "Think hard and tell me anything you remember, even if it doesn't seem important."

Rosie had her eyes shut, trying to think, when

the officer said, "Here he comes. Stay here while I talk to him."

Gladly Rosie thought. She turned and watched out the rear window of the patrol car.

Benny looked for Rosie as he ran. He paid no attention to the car parked on the other side of the road.

The officer, gun drawn, approached Benny.

"Police," the officer said. "Put your hands in the air."

Benny stopped, squinting in surprise. Slowly he put his hands above his head and waited while the officer made sure he had no weapons. Benny knew from his years of karate and boxing experience not to make his move too soon. Timing was everything.

"What's your name?" the officer asked as he slid the gun back in the holster.

Benny's boot kicked sharply forward, catching the officer in the stomach. At the same time he formed a fist with his right hand and brought it up hard, hitting the officer under his chin.

Rosie gasped.

The officer hit the ground hard and lay still. Benny yanked the gun out of the holster.

Rosie had seen the officer call on a two-way radio. She grabbed the microphone he had used.

"Help!" she said. "Send help!" She got no response. Had anyone heard her?

She saw a cellular phone and dialed 911. Nothing happened. She had never used a cellular phone. Was she supposed to press some other button, in addition to the numbers?

She looked over her shoulder again. This time Benny was walking toward the police car with the gun in his hand. She didn't have time to try to figure out the telephone.

Rosie locked the doors. She wished she knew how to drive; the engine was running.

Maybe I could, she thought. Maybe I could drive just far enough to escape. She had watched other people drive. She knew where the gas pedal and the brakes were.

Quickly Rosie climbed into the driver's seat. On the panel of letters on the dashboard, the letter *P* was lit. *P* for *Park*, Rosie thought. She grabbed the shift handle and pulled. It didn't move. She lifted it toward her and pulled again. This time the handle moved, and the lighted letter on the dashboard changed from *P* to *D*.

A shiver of excitement tickled the back of her neck. *D* for *Drive*. She pushed her foot on the gas pedal. The engine raced, but the car did not move.

The emergency brake! He must have put on

the emergency brake. Rosie looked on the floor beside her, between the two seats, where the emergency brake was located in her mother's car. It wasn't there. She looked in front of her right knee. A black handle stuck out. It said, "Push button and turn." Rosie did; the car rolled forward a few inches.

The man with the gun was only a few yards from the police car now. Rosie gripped the steering wheel with both hands and, with her heart in her throat, stepped on the gas again. This time the police car jerked forward off the shoulder and onto the road.

Rosie turned on the headlights. The car went across the center line, into the left lane. Rosie turned the steering wheel to the right, but she pulled too far. The car crossed the road and headed toward the ditch.

Rosie took her foot off the gas pedal and pulled the steering wheel left, not as hard this time. As the car straightened out, heading down the road, a shot rang out.

The noise exploded in Rosie's ears followed instantly by a second noise as the bullet hit the roof of the police car. He's shooting at me! Rosie realized. She pressed the gas pedal again, and the car went faster.

She looked in the rearview mirror. Benny was

running down the road, aiming the gun at the police car. Another shot rang out; the back windshield cracked into a spiderweb pattern.

Rosie looked away from the mirror and screamed. In the moment she had watched Benny instead of the road, the car had gone at an angle. Looming in front of her on the shoulder was a green road sign.

Her foot stomped hard on the brake pedal just before the right front fender of the police car smashed into the sign.

The car shuddered to a stop. Rosie turned off the engine.

Seconds later Benny stood beside the car. "Open the door," he demanded.

Rosie's hands shook as she reached for the door handle.

He stood there with the gun in his hand, staring at her as if wondering what to do next.

Behind him, she saw that the officer was on his feet, rubbing his chin. He walked quietly toward Benny.

"I never drove a car before," Rosie said, hoping her voice would cover any sound of the officer's footsteps. "My first effort and I smash up a cop car. They'll probably never let me get a driver's license now."

"Take off your shoes," Benny said.

"What?"

"You heard me. Take your shoes off and throw them out of the car."

Rosie untied her sneakers and tossed them onto the pavement.

"Now take off your socks and throw them out."

Rosie did it.

"Get in the other seat."

Rosie returned to the passenger's seat. She continued to talk, hoping Benny would not hear the officer approach. She babbled on about trying to drive, not sure if she was even making sense.

The officer was only ten feet away when Benny spun around and aimed the gun at him. The officer put his hands in the air.

"You," Benny said to the police officer, "are going to walk away from me now. Keep walking, with your hands in the air."

"I already called for help," the officer said. "You'll never get away."

"I will if anyone wants this kid to live."

The officer took a few steps down the road, his hands reaching for the stars.

"Faster," Benny said.

The officer walked faster.

Benny slid behind the steering wheel, started the engine, and shifted into reverse. The car eased backward. The road sign's metal post stayed bent over like a gymnast doing a backbend.

Benny shifted again and the car pulled from the shoulder onto the road.

I can't jump out again, Rosie thought. Not when he has a gun.

The police car, with Rosie trembling on the front seat, turned around and headed for town. Benny tapped the horn once as they passed the police officer. Then he quickly picked up speed.

"Where are we going?" Rosie asked.

"I am going to surprise my partner and relieve him of some money."

He held the gun with his right hand and steered with his left.

"And you," he said to Rosie, "are going with me. But first, you're going to go for a walk in the desert. On some long, sharp cactus spines."

Chapter

11

Elisabeth, her leg in a splint, was carried on a stretcher toward the ambulance. Her eyes drooped shut; the pain medication that the medics gave her made her sleepy.

Mrs. Lynwood, weeping and wringing her hands, asked if she could ride in the ambulance with her daughter. The medics exchanged quick glances.

"Your daughter's in shock," one of them said as they loaded Elisabeth into the ambulance. "It would be better for you to follow us."

"I'll get the car," Mr. Lynwood said. "We'll be right behind you."

"Bring the phone," Mrs. Lynwood said. "I want to call Mother."

A dozen other people milled around the road

near the NATURE TRAIL sign. They had seen the flashing lights and come to watch. Mrs. Saunders talked to everyone, hoping someone had seen Rosie and Kayo and might have a clue to what had happened to them.

"I talked to those girls this afternoon," one man said, "about a lost kitten."

"I remember them, too," a woman said. "Such nice girls, they were, and so concerned about the kitty."

Everyone there had talked to Kayo and Rosie.

None of them knew where the girls were now.

As the ambulance, followed by the Lynwoods' Thunderbird, drove off, one man said to Mr. Saunders, "Awhile ago someone in the campsite across from me honked a horn. It was fast and steady for just a couple of seconds, not a light *beep-beep* the way you'd warn a bicyclist or kids playing in the road, but a real hard honking. You know what I mean?"

Mr. Saunders nodded.

"Seemed unusual for a campground," the man continued. "People are generally considerate about noise, especially once it starts to get dark. Anyway, I turned on my outside lights and looked out just as a camper pulled away. I didn't think anything more about it at the time; I as-sumed they had come to pick someone up and honked the horn to let the person know they were there. But now that I think back, it pulled out of the campsite of those people whose girl broke her leg."

"What kind of camper was it?" Mr. Saunders asked.

The man shrugged. "Beats me. I looked out just as it drove off. Looked like one of those pickups with a camper added on the back, but I couldn't swear to it. Probably doesn't have anything to do with your girls, anyway. Just thought I'd mention it. Seemed strange that the folks whose girl got hurt were in the same campsite where the honking was earlier."

It does seem strange, Mr. Saunders thought. Too strange. A horn being honked loudly and fast might have been someone trying to signal for help. And Kayo's hat was on the ground, in that same campsite.

He hoped the police would hurry.

Kayo could tell that the truck was now in town. The engine noise was quieter and the truck idled occasionally, as if waiting for a traffic light to change. She heard other cars and knew they were now in heavier traffic.

She tried to climb on the bench again, this time on the street side, so she could signal those

other cars. It was impossible to keep her balance
with the truck starting and stopping. Every time
she got on her knees and tried to wriggle up on
the bench, the truck jerked forward and she toppled over.

Her arms ached from being tied behind her
back. This is probably ruining my pitching arm
forever, she thought. I'll never strike out another
batter. Of course, if she didn't get away from her
captor, it might not matter whether she could
pitch or not. She might not ever play baseball
again.

She lay still a moment, trying to think. She
knew the truck would stop eventually. The men
must have some destination.

Big money, here we come, the man had said.
He talked as if he expected someone to pay him
for kidnapping her.

They took the wrong girl! The realization hit
Kayo like a wild pitch. They expect to collect a
ransom for Elisabeth, and they took the wrong girl!

Now what? she wondered. When they find out
who I am, what will they do? Try to collect
money from Mom?

She pictured her mother, in tears, receiving a
telephone call that demanded money. She wondered if the men would call her dad, too. Fat

chance that Dad would pay a ransom; he wouldn't even pay for baseball camp.

They can threaten to kill me, Kayo thought bitterly, and he probably won't even care.

The pickup truck slowed and then stopped. The engine quit running.

We're here, Kayo thought. Wherever it is that they're taking me, we've arrived.

Rosie huddled against the door of the police car, watching Benny drive.

He still held the gun in his right hand, resting lightly on his leg, while he steered with his left hand.

Rosie had watched movies where the bad guy drove off with a hostage. She always liked those scary scenes when the driver glanced across the front seat at the victim.

But this isn't a movie, she thought, where you know everything will turn out all right in the end. This is real, and there are no guarantees of a happy ending.

They passed the place where Rosie had jumped out of the camper. She glimpsed the big cholla she had hidden behind. To her relief, he said nothing more about a barefoot walk in the desert.

They left the fields of cacti and entered a commercial area. A fruit stand, tent flaps drawn for the night, huddled on the corner. An orange cat streaked across the road in front of them.

The police radio crackled to life. Rosie jumped at the sudden sound. "Car Fourteen. Car Fourteen. What is your position?"

Rosie looked at Benny, wondering what he would do. Benny glared at the radio.

"Maybe this is Car Fourteen," Rosie said.

The radio spoke again. "Car Fourteen. Respond, please. What is your position?"

Rosie clutched the edge of the seat and waited.

Benny pushed his foot on the gas, as if by driving faster he could get away from the radio.

She felt for a seat belt and buckled it on.

And then, ahead of them, coming toward them, she saw headlights and flashing blue lights. Rosie held her breath as they approached. There were two sets of lights.

Benny pushed the gas pedal to the floor. They shot forward, past the two police cars.

Immediately sirens shrilled.

Rosie looked back. One police car kept going; the other spun around and followed Benny.

Benny laid the gun on his lap and grabbed the steering wheel with both hands. He turned right at the next corner; the tires squealed and the car tipped on its side, riding on only two wheels.

We're going to tip over, Rosie thought. He's

going too fast; he can't control the car. We're going to crash!

The patrol car bounced slightly as the other two tires touched down again. They sped forward.

"You might as well stop," Rosie said. "You'll never get away, now that the police have seen you. Every police car in Phoenix will be here soon. They'll put up road blocks."

"I'll get away," Benny said.

"They'll shoot you."

"No, they won't. Not when you're with me. They won't take a chance on hitting you."

Rosie knew he was right.

The siren continued and the flashing lights swirled through the windows as the police car followed.

The sirens were in stereo now, and Rosie knew other patrol cars had joined the chase, approaching from different directions.

I'm surrounded by police, Rosie thought, but they won't be able to help me. Not when Benny has a gun.

She stared at the black handgun on Benny's lap. Rosie disliked guns of any kind—what were they good for, except to kill?

I need to get the gun, Rosie thought. If I can get the gun away from him, he'll have to surrender.

She knew she would not actually use the gun. She would never shoot another person. Much as she disliked the man beside her, she did not want to take his whole future—possibly fifty or sixty more years of living—away from him.

But if she could get the gun, she would remove his biggest threat.

With the gun, and Rosie as a hostage, he was in control. Without the gun, he wouldn't stand a chance of getting away.

Moving her right hand slowly, she opened her window half way. He either didn't notice or didn't care.

She edged sideways on her seat toward him, twisting her upper body as if looking over her left shoulder. In reality she was watching him, waiting for her chance.

She leaned toward Benny, close enough to smell his sweaty odor. She heard his breath coming fast, as if he were still running. He's scared, Rosie realized. He knows he's surrounded.

Every nerve in Rosie's body was alert. Her pulse pounded in her throat as she waited for a chance to grab the gun.

Chapter

12

*B*enny jammed on the brakes. The tires complained loudly.

Rosie braced her bare feet against the floorboard and faced front again to see why he was stopping. Two police cars, parked nose to nose, blocked the road in front of them.

Benny clutched the wheel, cursing. He looked in the rearview mirror and swore again.

Rosie held her breath.

Now!

She lunged sideways and snatched the gun from Benny's lap.

"Hey!" he yelled. He reached over and tried to grab her arm, but the rear of the car was skidding, and he couldn't steer and fight with her at the same time. He yanked on the steering wheel with both hands.

Rosie threw the gun out the open window, flinging it as hard as she could. As the car screeched to a stop, she saw the gun land in some scraggly weeds at the side of the road.

Benny made half a U-turn and stopped. The police car behind them was parked crossways, blocking most of the street. Another police car rolled up beside it and stopped. A police officer jumped out. She crouched behind the first car, a gun in her hand.

Benny's head turned rapidly from front to back to front, as if he were watching a tennis match. Then he slumped against the seat and turned off the ignition.

Rosie opened the door, got out, and ran to the closest police car. The gun she had thrown out the window was quickly found on the side of the road.

Rosie listened while Benny talked to the police.

"I'll tell you everything," Benny said. "I'm not taking the blame alone when it was all Jasper's idea. No way." He told the police Jasper's plan and the name of the company where Jasper had rented the camper. "Will I get a shorter sentence," he asked, "because I told you about Jasper?"

"I can't promise anything," the officer said.

"At least I won't be the only one who gets caught."

"Where did he take the other girl?" the officer asked.

Benny shrugged. "A motel. He was going to get a motel room and call Mr. Lynwood from there."

A police officer questioned Rosie, too, and then drove her back to camp. As they rode, Rosie wondered how many hundreds of motels there were in the Phoenix area. The chance of finding the one Kayo was in seemed impossible.

When the camper stopped, Kayo lay on the floor, listening.

The pickup door slammed.

They'll take me out of this camper soon, Kayo thought. When they do, how can I get away?

With the truck stopped, she was able to hoist herself up on the bench again. She looked out the window at a yellow neon sign: BENCHMARK MOTEL. Below the big yellow letters, smaller red letters announced: VACANCY.

The man had parked at the far end of the parking lot, away from other vehicles. Unless a motel guest went jogging or walked a dog, it was unlikely that anyone would come close enough to see Kayo's face and realize she needed help.

How else could she attract attention? Try as

she might, Kayo could think of no way to save herself. Alone in the back of the camper, she watched and waited.

Jasper registered for a room, using yet another name. Again, he paid in cash.

Jasper had planned to wait a few hours before making the phone call. He wanted to give Mr. Lynwood time to worry. He wanted him to think about what might happen to his daughter.

He found his room and went in. He kept fingering the bottom of his T-shirt. He shifted from one foot to the other, unable to stand still. What if the other girl called the cops? What if the cops found Benny and Benny talked? Jasper decided not to wait. He would call right now and get it over with.

He had to bring the girl inside before he called. Her father might demand to speak to her, as proof that Jasper really had her.

As Jasper walked across the dark parking lot, memories of prison pushed into his mind. He knew what would happen if he got caught.

He moved the pickup to the parking space closest to his room. He backed into the parking place and got out.

He stood at the back of the camper for a moment before he unlocked the door. He looked around to be sure no one was watching out a window or buying a soda from the vending machine that was two doors down from his room.

It will soon be over, he told himself. Relax. By this time tomorrow he'd have the money and be on his way to Mexico.

Satisfied that he was not being observed, he unlocked the door of the camper.

Kayo was on the bench with her head under the curtain.

Jasper stepped up into the camper and pulled her from the bench onto his shoulder. He squatted in the door for an instant, looked both ways, and then sat down and slid to the pavement.

He quickly carried her into the motel room and set her on the bed.

Jasper looked hard at Kayo. He had seen Elisabeth Lynwood twice, from a distance, at the company picnics before Andrew Lynwood fired him. Kids grow up fast. They change. But he remembered the long, blond hair. And she was still on the skinny side.

Kayo returned the man's gaze, noticing the details so she could describe him later. About six feet tall. Dark hair, in need of a trim. Early thirties. A brass belt buckle shaped like a truck.

Jasper walked to the far side of the bed and sat down on it, with his back to Kayo. He reached for the telephone on the bedside table and dialed the number of Andrew Lynwood's cellular phone. It had not been easy to get that personal phone number. Jasper, pretending to have urgent business with Mr. Lynwood, had tricked one of the secretaries at Lynwood Computer into giving it to him.

As the telephone rang, he closed his eyes and pictured Andrew Lynwood, in his fancy motor home, reaching to pick it up.

"Hello. Andrew Lynwood here." The voice sounded exactly the way Jasper remembered it. I've waited a long time for this, Jasper thought.

In a husky, false voice Jasper said the speech he had rehearsed dozens of times in the last week. "I have your daughter. If you want to see her alive, have one hundred thousand dollars in unmarked cash ready by noon tomorrow. You will receive instructions on where to take it. Do not call the police."

There was a moment of silence at the other end of the line. Jasper smiled, imagining the panic on Andrew Lynwood's face. Who's the winner now? he thought, recalling how Mr. Lynwood had testified against him at the trial. He imagined Mr. Lynwood trying to compose himself, to control his emotions enough to answer.

When Andrew Lynwood spoke, however, his voice was strong and firm. "You are lying," he said.

Jasper, taken by surprise by this response, said nothing. He turned and looked at the girl. Was she Elisabeth? Or was she a kid who resembled Elisabeth and who just happened to be running toward the Lynwood's motor home?

Mr. Lynwood spoke again. "My daughter is in a hospital bed," he said, "not three feet away from me."

Jasper hung up.

He opened the drawer of the bedside table, removed a telephone directory, and turned to Hospitals in the Yellow Pages. There were three: Mesa General, Mesa Lutheran, and Southside.

He dialed the first one listed.

"Mesa General Hospital."

"Do you have a patient there named Elisabeth Lynwood?" Jasper asked.

"One moment, please."

Jasper tapped his fingers nervously on the open phone book. Andrew Lynwood was probably just stalling for time, hoping to get a recorder on the telephone before Jasper called back, but Jasper had to be sure.

The voice on the telephone spoke again. "She hasn't been assigned a room yet," the voice said, "so I can't connect you. She was admitted to Emergency less than an hour ago."

Jasper slammed the receiver down and turned

to the girl. "You are not Elisabeth Lynwood, are you?"

Kayo shook her head.

Jasper put his face in his hands. He felt like a balloon that had just been pricked with a pin; all the energy was seeping out of him and vanishing into the air along with the ransom. Goodbye, one hundred thousand dollars. Andrew Lynwood had won again.

After the first few seconds of shock, anger exploded and Jasper jumped to his feet. He picked up one of the clear glasses that sat next to an ice bucket on the dresser and threw it across the room. It hit the wall, near the bathroom door, and shattered.

Perched on the edge of the bed, Kayo waited and watched. She felt a momentary sense of satisfaction at seeing the man so distraught.

Jasper heaved the second glass after the first one, smashing it in the same spot.

Then he stopped, and looked hard at Kayo. "You are Elisabeth Lynwood's friend," he said. "If her friend is in trouble, Elisabeth will want to help, won't she?" Jasper rubbed his hands together nervously. "I wonder how much that friendship is worth," he said. "Five thousand? Ten thousand?" He was talking to himself, as if Kayo weren't there. "If Elisabeth cries, and begs

Daddy to help, the wrong kid might even be worth twenty thousand."

He went into the bathroom. As soon as he shut the door, Kayo rolled across the bed. She sat up by the telephone, and using her head, she nudged the receiver off the holder so it lay on the bedside table.

Kayo bent over the receiver until her nose was over number nine. Her eyes crossed when she was so close, but she pressed nine and heard the click. Then she found number one and pressed it twice with her nose. *Click. Click.*

Kayo heard the toilet flush and the sound of water running. Faintly she heard a voice on the telephone. She put her lips close to the receiver and groaned.

The bathroom door opened. Kayo rolled over, facing away from the telephone, hoping he wouldn't notice that it was off the hook.

Trace the call, Kayo thought. *Get the address and send help before he notices the telephone.*

Jasper came out of the bathroom. "Okay," he said. "Let's call him again."

I have to distract him, Kayo thought. I have to keep him from seeing the telephone. She moaned loudly.

He looked at her.

Kayo moaned again, hoping she would also be heard on the other end of the telephone line.

Ignoring her groans, he walked to the telephone and saw the receiver lying on the table. He picked it up, put it to his ear, and listened a second.

"Cancel the call," he said. "It's a mistake." He waited a moment and then said, "That's right. There's no problem here. My baby was playing with the phone."

He hung up and glared at Kayo. "I don't have to let them find you alive," he said. "I can collect the ransom and then do whatever I want with you."

Chapter

*J*asper's eyes blazed with anger.

Kayo shuddered.

"We can't stay here," he said. "Thanks to your phone call, I'll have to drive awhile and make my next call from a different place."

We can't leave, Kayo thought. Maybe her call was traced. Maybe the emergency operator was suspicious of Jasper's explanation about a baby. Maybe help was on the way.

Kayo moaned as loudly as she could and rolled her head from side to side.

"Cut that out."

She moaned again. She had to stall. She had to keep him here as long as possible.

"If this is some kind of trick," he said, "you'll regret it." Cautiously he removed the gag from Kayo's mouth.

"I need to go to the bathroom," she said.

"You'll have to wait."

"I can't wait. I have to go really bad." If he untied her to let her go to the bathroom, she could shut the bathroom door and lock herself in. "Please," she said.

"No. We have to get out of here."

"If you don't let me use the bathroom, I'll wet on you when you pick me up."

The man glared at her for a second, and then he untied her and led her to the bathroom.

With her heart in her throat Kayo reached for the door.

"The door stays open," he said. He put his foot in the doorway so she couldn't close it. "I'll stand here."

The last thing Kayo wanted to do was use the bathroom with him standing there, but if she didn't, he'd know she had tried to trick him. Slowly she unbuckled her belt.

Someone banged loudly on the door.

They both froze.

"Police! Open up!"

"You're my daughter," Jasper whispered. "You got that? My partner has your friend in the next room. If you want to see her again, you tell the cops you're my kid and we're on vacation."

Kayo nodded. Was he telling her the truth? Was Rosie in the next room, with the other man?

Jasper hurried to the window and pulled the drapes open slightly. Kayo followed him and looked out.

Two police cars, lights flashing, were parked behind the pickup. Officers with guns drawn stood beside it.

Jasper slammed his fist against the wall.

The police banged on the door again.

Jasper unlocked the door and opened it. "Good evening, officer," he said.

"Jasper Dodge," the officer said, "you are under arrest. You have the right to remain silent—"

"I am not Jasper Dodge," Jasper interrupted him. "My daughter and I were just—"

"Save it for the judge," the officer replied. "We have a full confession from your sidekick."

As the officer continued to read Jasper his rights, a second officer led Kayo to one of the patrol cars.

A different police officer knocked on the door of Rosie's motor home. "Your other girl is safe," the officer said when Mr. Saunders answered.

"Where is she?" Rosie asked.

Bone Breath pawed at the officer's pant leg. Phoenix, on the sofa, batted at Bone Breath's tail.

"She was found in a motel room in Mesa after an alert emergency operator traced a suspicious call. She's bruised from bouncing around in the back of the camper with her hands and feet tied, but she doesn't appear to have any serious injuries. She's being taken to Mesa General's emergency room to be examined."

"We have written permission from her mother for Kayo to have medical treatment," Mrs. Saunders said.

"Can you direct me to the hospital?" Mr. Saunders said.

"I'll take you there, if you like," the officer said. "I imagine it's a bit hard to drive a vehicle like this in a strange city at night. Especially with animals pestering you."

He looked down. Bone Breath pawed his pant leg again.

"Bone Breath," said Rosie, "stop that."

Bone Breath wagged his tail and licked the officer's shoe.

"We would be grateful for a ride," Mr. Saunders said.

When they arrived at the hospital, Rosie and her parents rushed in the door of the emergency ward. A nurse led them into a large room full of beds separated by long curtains.

"A doctor has already examined her," the nurse said. "There are no serious injuries."

"What a relief," Mrs. Saunders said.

"Your family is here, Kayo," the nurse said as she pulled aside the third curtain.

Kayo jumped off the bed when she saw them. They all hugged Kayo at the same time. Everyone began to talk at once, stopped, laughed, and talked at the same time again. Mrs. Saunders wiped tears from her cheeks, and Mr. Saunders kept saying, "You're all right," as if he couldn't believe it.

"We need one of you to sign some papers at the admitting desk," the nurse said.

"I'll do it," Mrs. Saunders said. She left.

"Are your girls twins?" the nurse asked Mr. Saunders.

Rosie and Kayo laughed.

"I wish they were," Mr. Saunders said, "but they aren't related. Kayo is our honorary second daughter." He hugged her again.

Kayo smiled at him, her eyes shining. *Our honorary second daughter.* He truly cares about me, Kayo thought. He likes to be with me. He is all the things my own father is not. And I care about him, too. I love both Mr. and Mrs. Saunders—not the way I love Mom, but a different, special kind of love.

A warmth spread through Kayo as she realized she had a substitute father. With that realization, she let go of the resentment she felt toward her own dad. She would always regret that he did not choose to be a part of her life, but she would no longer waste her energy wishing he would change. Instead, she would enjoy her status as an "honorary second daughter."

A doctor came in and said, "Your girl had a terrible shock. It would be wise to keep her here for twenty-four hours, just for observation."

"Twenty-four hours!" Kayo said. "I can't stay here for twenty-four hours. I'd miss the ball game."

The doctor raised her eyebrows. "Which is more important," she said, "a ball game or your health?"

"If I have to miss spring training," Kayo said, "I *will* go into shock. I'll have a heart attack! I'll hyperventilate! I'll fall down dead right in the middle of the floor. I'll—"

"The baseball game means a lot to Kayo," Mr. Saunders cut in.

"So I see," said the doctor.

"Unless there is a compelling medical reason to keep her here," Mr. Saunders said, "we'll take her with us."

"Let's go," said Kayo.

Before leaving the hospital, they stopped to see Elisabeth. Her parents were there, too.

"I'll have the cast on for six weeks," Elisabeth said, "but I get to go home tomorrow."

"If Elisabeth hadn't broken her leg," Mr. Lynwood said, "she would have been kidnapped instead of Kayo, and I would have paid the ransom. You girls saved me a bundle of money, and, as a small thank you, I want to give each of you a gift."

He took a bulging money clip from his pocket and removed two crisp one-hundred-dollar bills. He held them out, one to Rosie and one to Kayo.

"That isn't necessary," Mrs. Saunders said.

Kayo crossed her fingers. Please let me take it, she thought. Please, please, please.

"These girls endured a terrible ordeal because of their friendship with Elisabeth," Mr. Lynwood said.

"It's kind of you to offer," Mr. Saunders said, "but we cannot allow the girls to accept."

Mr. Lynwood put the bills back in his money clip.

That would have paid for baseball camp, Kayo thought, but all she said was, "Thanks, anyway."

Mrs. Saunders called Kayo's mom from the hospital, as soon as the discharge papers were signed, and told her what had happened. "We didn't want you to hear it on the news or read it in the paper," Mrs. Saunders said. Kayo assured her mother that she was unharmed.

Rosie and Kayo talked nonstop all the way back to Usery Mountain Recreation Area, filling each other in on what had happened as well as answering a few questions from the police officer who drove them.

When they got back to the motor home, it looked as if it had snowed inside. While they were gone, Phoenix had unrolled and shredded all the toilet tissue; mounds of white covered the floor. Bone Breath, drooling with excitement at this new game, ran back and forth with bits of moist tissue clinging to his beard.

Rosie and Kayo kept talking while they cleaned up the mess. They talked while they got ready for bed. And after they climbed into their sleeping bags, and settled Phoenix and Bone Breath between them, they lay in the dark, still talking.

It was two A.M. before they fell asleep.

It was five A.M. when Phoenix woke up. She jumped on Mr. Saunders's chest and licked his cheek. Mr. Saunders groaned. Phoenix meowed. Hearing the cat, Bone Breath barked.

"This cat," muttered Mr. Saunders, "has to go. Today."

* * *

The ball game was everything Kayo had dreamed it would be, and more. Mrs. Saunders bought her a souvenir cap, and Mr. Saunders played the scoreboard's Baseball Trivia game with her. She loved being an honorary daughter.

"This was the best day of my whole life," Kayo said as they walked across the parking lot after the game ended.

When they opened the motor home door, they discovered that Phoenix and Bone Breath had entertained themselves with Act Two of the Great Toilet Tissue Play.

"Next stop, animal shelter," said Mr. Saunders as they gathered the shredded paper and stuffed it in a garbage sack.

"Dad!" Rosie cried. "You promised we could try again tonight. There are still people in camp that we haven't talked to. Maybe one of them wants a kitten."

"Your father is only joking," Mrs. Saunders said.

"I can't joke. I'm too cranky from lack of sleep," Mr. Saunders said. "I have been up since five, thanks to a certain cat."

As soon as they got back to Usery Mountain, Rosie and Kayo walked Bone Breath. Mr. and Mrs. Wilbert were sitting in their lawn chairs again. She wore the same locket.

"There you are!" Mrs. Wilbert said, jumping up and coming to greet them. "We've been watching for you."

"That's right," Mr. Wilbert said. "We talked all day about that kitten you found, and we decided maybe we're ready to love another cat, after all."

"We'd like to come and see it," Mrs. Wilbert said.

"You can come right now," Rosie said.

When they approached the motor home, Phoenix sat on the back of the sofa, looking out the window.

"Why, she does look like Bumpkins!" Mrs. Wilbert cried. Inside, she gathered Phoenix into her arms and buried her face in the kitten's furry neck. Phoenix purred and snuggled closer. When Mrs. Wilbert looked up, there were tears in her eyes. "It feels so good," she said, "to hold a little cat again."

Mr. Wilbert patted her shoulder. "Now, now, Mother," he said, "don't get all weepy on me." He stroked the kitten's head. "It looks to me," he said, "as if this cat needs a home, and we have a home that needs a cat."

"Does she have a name?" Mrs. Wilbert asked.

"We call her Phoenix, but you can name her whatever you want," Kayo said.

"Phoenix," Mrs. Wilbert said. "Yes, I like that.

113

She is rising from the ashes of abandonment to her new life as our darling pet. Let's call her Phoenix."

Kayo frowned. Rosie and her parents and now the Wilberts all knew the legend about the phoenix bird. Did everyone in the whole world know Greek mythology, except her?

Maybe I should read more, she thought, and pay attention to Rosie's vocabulary words.

"We'll need to buy a few things for her before we take her with us," Mr. Wilbert said.

Mrs. Saunders said, "She comes complete with litter box, a bag of litter, a scooper, food, and a toy mouse. We bought it all this morning, on our way to the ball game."

Mr. Wilbert carried the equipment. Mrs. Wilbert carried Phoenix. "We'll need a scratching post," Mr. Wilbert said as they started down the road. "And some of those fuzzy rainbow balls that Bumpkins always liked."

In a voice low enough that only Rosie heard, Kayo added, "And a few dozen rolls of toilet paper."

When Kayo arrived home at the end of the trip, her mother greeted her with a surprise.

"I got a bonus at work," Mrs. Benton said, "for the best employee suggestion of the year. I used part of it to pay for Baseball Camp. The registration form was in your room and your coach said it wasn't too late to sign up."

Kayo hugged her mother.

Mrs. Benton smiled at Kayo. "It's good to have you home. I missed you."

"I missed you, too, but it was a great vacation. We even had a Care Club project."

"Care Club," said Rosie, "helped a homeless animal. Again."

"Care Club," said Mr. Saunders, "scared us out of our wits. Again."

About the Author

Peg Kehret's popular novels for young people are regularly nominated for state awards. She has received the Young Hoosier Award, the Golden Sower Award, the Iowa Children's Choice Award, the Sequoyah Award, the Celebrate Literacy Award, and the Pacific Northwest Young Reader's Choice Award, the Maude Hart Lovelace Award, and the New Mexico Land of Enchantment Award. She lives with her husband, Carl, and their animal friends in Washington State, where she is a volunteer at the Humane Society and SPCA. Her two grown children and four grandchildren live in Washington, too.

Peg's Minstrel titles include *Nightmare Mountain; Sisters, Long Ago; Cages; Terror at the Zoo; Horror at the Haunted House;* and the *Frightmares*™ series.